T0167736

WHERE THERE ARE MONSTERS

BREANNE MC IVOR

WHERE THERE ARE MONSTERS

PEEPAL TREE

First published in Great Britain in 2019
Peepal Tree Press Ltd
17 King's Avenue
Leeds LS6 1QS
England

ISBN13: 9781845234362

Supported using public funding by
ARTS COUNCIL
ENGLAND

Thrice he assayed, and thrice, in spite of scorn,
Tears, such as Angels weep, burst forth: at last
Words interwove with sighs found out their way.

John Milton, *Paradise Lost*

For my mother, with love

CONTENTS

Where There Are Monsters

Where We Are Monsters

WHERE THERE ARE MONSTERS

OPHELIA

Ophelia's words are tinkling in my ears. They smell like cut grass just washed with rain. I want to breathe her. Strip her. Peel her skin and get to the heart of the woman buried under her layers of poise.

We are at rehearsal in the sprawling National Academy for the Performing Arts. The empty red seats roll back in waves before us. Ophelia is on her cell phone.

I wait until she hangs up. "Ophelia?"

"Yes?"

I want to lean forward and press my fingers on the hardness of her collarbone before pulling her plump bottom lip between my teeth.

"Marcus?"

"Yes?"

"You called me?"

"Oh, yes."

She sits on the stage, script spread out before her with all her lines highlighted in yellow. She is not wearing stage make-up but she already looks like the lead actress.

How could a woman named Ophelia not be an actress? I wish we were performing Hamlet. She would be herself, of course, peering out at me from the wings.

I can hear myself. *To be or not to be – that is the question.*

My words are the choking smoke that heralds the start of a fire. *Whether 'tis nobler in mind to suffer –*

"Marcus?"

"Sorry."

Ophelia's forehead crumples.

"I was wondering if you wanted to meet to brainstorm on Saturday?" I ask. "I still think we can work on our first scene together?"

Ophelia whips out her phone, finds her calendar. The light illuminates her face as she opens it. "What time on Saturday?"

"One?" I say, hoping. *Please, God. Give me this. Give me an hour with this woman in a coffee shop. Give me her hair, twisted into ringlets that sink into one another. Give me the stomach-shudder when her shirt slips off her shoulder and I see her flesh crossed by a bra strap. Give me –*

"Can you do one-thirty?"

I can do anything you want.

"Marcus?"

"Yes, of course – Jardin in the mall?" I try to say this as if I am the type who goes to Jardin des Tuileries instead of Tecla's vegetable stand where I haggle over the price of an avocado.

"Sure," Ophelia says. "That sounds like a treat."

Would she taste my desperation if we kissed – that sour, morning-after taste that I can never brush out of my mouth? I won't mess it up; I won't think crazy thoughts – all mixed metaphors and fantasies while I remain tongue-tied.

"Great," I say. "I'm looking forward to it."

Ophelia tucks her curls behind one pixie-pointed ear. Touching her would feel like the sun hitting my face first thing in the morning.

Already my head-voices are telling me that this is madness. How could somebody like Ophelia ever want anything to do with me? She probably rolled her eyes when she saw my name on the cast list.

Ophelia smiles – more a lifting of the lips – before returning to her script.

Our director wants us to spend time reading the lines, and living the characters before we begin performing, but I can already see her weaving her character's clothes over her own. Her pink dress – which only a moment before was elegantly gathered around her wasp-waist – seems to hang off her frame as if she has made herself thinner.

I return to my script and try to ignore her. I imagine my character as he is portrayed in Act One: young, grasping – a ghetto youth determined to claw his way out. Not such a hard thing for me. I even look the part – dark and scrawny, like a weed springing up from a pavement crack.

★

I'd first visited this theatre as a secondary school student. My mother was in between jobs, and someone had stolen the government-sponsored boxed lunch that was supposed to prevent boys like me from going hungry. My stomach was lashed with acid. It was as if I was reduced to this single need. Eat. Eat. Eat.

That first time at the theatre, my nostrils quivered as they inhaled beef patties being seared in the cafeteria. The programme was on my lap, but in the dimness, the only word I could discern was the play's title: *Steel*. The tenor steelpan, glittering on the front cover, looked like a pizza. The indentations that formed the notes could have been pepperoni.

I trailed my tongue along my wrist to lick the salt from my sweat.

And then the bright lights winked and popped and the steelpans – hidden in the pit beneath the stage – rumbled. My emotions ebbed and flowed with the tenor pans. The guitar pans were like fingers strumming my vocal chords. I didn't even realise I was humming until a classmate shouted, "Oh God, man, hush your stink mouth!"

But even he could not pull me away. The crimson curtains rose and Winston Spree Simon was sitting on stage reading a newspaper. I even forgot it was an actor since the real Spree Simon was long dead. He was so engrossed, I wanted to know what the headline was. I had never seen such arrow-like focus.

The play was a love story between an African man and an Indian woman. When they first touched, I felt it in my marrow; and when the racial tensions threatened to smash their love to pieces, my indignation fell in droplets down my face. I wanted to sweep the characters into my arms and save them.

Then it was over.

After that, there was only one job for me – acting.

★

After rehearsal, Ophelia saunters over to her new Honda Civic. "Can I drop you somewhere?" she asks.

I imagine Ophelia driving into my neighbourhood, leaving behind the two-storey houses with landscaped lawns, forcing her car down narrowing streets with corner stores jutting off the pavement, men smoking outside bars, whistling at her.

"It's OK, thanks," I say.

"All right, Marcus. See you Saturday." She leaves with one last pop of her horn.

I stand on the pavement, stick my thumb out and wait. A taxi with a dented fender screeches to a stop.

"Diego?"

"How deep in Diego Martin you going?"

"Quarry Street."

"I not going that far in."

He drops me at the bottom of my hill in front of Tecla's vegetable stand. The swollen pawpaws on her wooden table make my stomach contract. Still, now isn't the time to spend money. I've heard that a coffee in Jardin can cost $25.

"You buying, or you just drooling on my fruits?" Tecla asks.

"Just drooling," I say.

"Well, you go have to drool another time because it looks like it go rain." Tecla hauls the table into her small shop.

Halfway to my house, the downpour starts and the galvanised roofs play their most popular song. *Plink. Plink.* The droplets find their way inside my shirt collar and merge with the sweat on my back.

Plink. Plink – Who the hell do you think you are, Marcus Blackman? Asking a girl like Ophelia on a date?

It's not a date. It's a brainstorming session.

Liar!

Plink.

I'm not a liar.

Plink.

Liar.

Plunk.

I see our biggest metal pot nestled between clumps of brown, desiccated grass. Who put it out there? It's too early for my mother to be home.

"What happened?" I ask.

"You know we eh have no water for a week. I collecting rain water," she says.

In the kitchen, she is kneading dough. We both know that I don't give a rat's ass about some stupid pot – with a bottom burned black from making too much pelau – sitting in the scrap of earth we call "the garden".

The clock behind the stove reads 3:35 p.m. She should be at the Gatcliffes, working.

"Why are you home?" I ask.

"Well, you see… we was very busy this week. The Mister had guests staying over. So in between making lunch and a bottle for the baby, I prop she up in the crib. I didn't leave she long. But Miss Gabrielle find she. She tell me some story about how the baby can't breathe, give me big speech about how is God who send she to she daughter…"

The words are sandpaper rubbing my skin. That Gatcliffe job pays eighteen dollars an hour and they let her take home food after the family has eaten.

I want to pull that blasted pot from the garden and smash our house to nothing. I want to tear at that part of my mother that thinks it is okay to leave a baby propped up in its crib.

Jesus, fuck. Don't I deserve at least one parent who isn't a total piece of shit?

"So I tell your father you will come down to he bar this Saturday coming. He say he go pay you twenty dollars an hour."

"This Saturday?"

"Marcus, I know you studying and already have that small work by Chin's at night, but just until I get something…"

"I'm busy this Saturday."

"You busy?"

"With my play."

"But you only getting paid for that after they sell tickets."

"Yes, but if I want to get paid at all I have to rehearse."

"Is just one Saturday. Tell them you sick."

I am sick. I want to rain cuss words on this churchgoing woman.

I try to hold on to Hamlet's lines and Ophelia's eyes when I walk up my hill. But it's hard to hold on to poetry when my head is crowded with, "Marcus, we have no water… Marcus, you done by Chin already? …Marcus, I fire the job."

Please, please-please, God! Give me this – just one date. Give me the chance to let go of this hill in Diego Martin for one hour.

★

The dry season is back , and one cheap plastic fan can't hold it at bay. The sweat slicking my back has made my T-shirt a second skin. I've been holding my phone for almost an hour.

Procrastinating.

Call him!

Rehearsing.

"Hey, Pops. Marcus here. Look, I can't make it this Saturday. I'm so sorry."

"Hey, Pops. Look, there's this girl…"

"Hey, Pops. It's your son. You made half of me. Do you have to make me work for $160? Can't you just give it to me because we need it…"

"Hey, Pops. I can do this Saturday but I need to take a long lunch break. 12:30 to 2:30…"

I need this. This is a woman who makes air lighter, who makes words brighter, who lifts lines so that a playwright isn't just a writer but a god. I squirrelled away dollar after dollar so that I could afford this. Give me this one thing.

Call him!

His phone rings.

Once.

Twice.

Please answer…

Another ring.

Please don't answer.

Fifth ring. "Hey, Pops. It's Marcus."

★

The bullets have opened a hundred eyes in the body and each one weeps blood. I peer through the lower corner of our curtain at the figure lying face-down on the road. All I can think is, *Did this bastard have to get shot on Saturday?*

The loss of a life is abstract when all you want is a woman – so badly, that you feel her even though you've never touched her. You taste your name in her mouth although she's never said it the way you want her to.

Probably another gangster anyway.

I pace in the kitchen as the clock ticks away. The heat has ironed our plastic tablecloth onto the table. It burns my fingertips, my scalp, the back of my throat…

I can't be late. I already begged my father to give me a two-hour lunch break. I can't come in a second after he expects me.

I should send Ophelia a message saying I can't make it. My grandfather had a stroke; my mother had an asthma attack.

These are problems she will understand. If I tell her I can't leave until the police cart a dead body off the road, or at least throw a white sheet over it while they interrogate the residents – none of whom have seen anything – she would probably call the director and demand a change of cast.

I told my father I would get there for eleven. I have to leave now, especially because word of the shooting would have spread, and taxis would stay clear of our area.

"All right. I'm going," I call to she of the no-job and no-savings.

"Now? You know you can't go nowhere."

"I'll be late."

She steps into the kitchen. "Marcus Blackman, you and I both know these men don't like witnesses. What if they think you meddling in their business? What if they think you going to the police, eh? What if they decide the easiest thing is to shut you up? Better you late than –"

"What do you want me to do?"

"I'll call your father. Ask him to lend us the money."

"I'm going." We both know that my father is not that type.

As I open the door, it is as if I'm swallowing a jar of coins. I never understood why the smell of blood leaves the taste of metal on your tongue. I push my hands into my pockets and look down. I know I can't look left or right. If someone is on the lookout for witnesses, I shouldn't appear too curious.

I'd spent the morning heating water on the stove so I could have a warm bucket-bath instead of splashing cold water under my arms and on my groin. I bet Ophelia's family have a couple tanks behind their house so they don't even realise when the water goes. I imagine Ophelia's naked feet as the droplets slip down her ankles and pool around her heels on the marble tiles.

And I, who made the effort to be fresh, am undone by the sun. Sweat soaks my armpits until when I'm finally at my father's bar, I'm sticky and late.

"Marko? You like your sleep too much, boy!" My father pushes a damp J-cloth into my hands. Chunks of carrot and what looks like chipped cashews are plastered to it.

"Moreno vomit on my toilet seat for the second week in a row," he says. "You come in time for the wipe up." He points his chin in the direction of the bathroom.

I should be sitting up in bed, learning my lines. Instead, I stoop beside the toilet and sweep the chunks of Moreno's stomach into the bowl and flush the toilet.

It is not yet midday, but it's Saturday and you could set your watch by the drunks who frequent this place. Sometimes, a sober man steps in who drinks just Coke. He will make his way to the backroom and sit, though I've never learnt – and wouldn't want to learn – what business my father transacts there.

The door of the stall swings open and cracks me on the back of my head. It's Brathwaite, the Bajan with the limp, who is always drunk by lunchtime.

"Markkkko," he says. "I thought you stop working here."

"Use the next stall, Brathwaite."

His fat fingers unbuckle his belt, and the tiny hooks of his zipper part. He flops out of his pants and piss is dripping from his member before he can angle it towards the toilet. I turn my face away but that can't stop the smell – like a fish at the market with the scales still on.

Brathwaite shakes himself, leaving yellow globules on my shoes.

"Your father say you acting." Brathwaite has a sneer in his voice. He stuffs himself back in his pants and lumbers off. I pull toilet paper from the roll and press it into my shoes.

Maybe I should have packed a change of clothes? Crept into the mall and passed wet wipes under my arms and along my back and shed this sweaty shirt and jeans.

"You taking your time today," my father says when I emerge from the bathroom.

"Brathwaite almost peed in my face."

"What the ass your face doing by Brathwaite cock?"

I say nothing.

"Squeeze out the cloth and wipe the tables," my father says.

I can't bring myself to run the same cloth over the counter. I wet another J-cloth and begin.

Eric Skerrit who – twenty years ago – sang a calypso that actually made it to the radio, is arguing with someone I cannot see across the bar. "Come over here and say that to my blasted face!" he shouts.

I step around him.

"Marko? What happen? You can't wipe where I sitting?"

I have to lean over him to wipe the table. The fatty flesh of his arm presses into my chest.

"You ever hear of the Lord Executioner?" he asks.

"Aren't you the Lord Executioner?"

"Damn right. Back in the day, I was the calypsonian to execute them all. But these youths, they don't know."

"It's a shame," I reply. What I want to say is, can you blame them for not knowing a drunk who had one hit song over the course of fifty years? I leave before he can start warbling his way through the scraps of his song that he still remembers.

Further down the bar, I come to a yellow lump crusted onto the counter and try to work it out with my nails.

"Like you're having a bad day."

I look up. It's Keron. He is wearing a white Calvin Klein polo and leaning against the bar drinking a Coke. I resume trying to force the crust off the counter and my nail splits.

Keron pulls out a switch blade. He flicks it open and scrapes the crust off with the tip.

"How much does he pay you?"

"Enough."

"Enough?"

"Yes. Enough."

"Good," he says. The ice in his Coke clinks as he drinks.

I keep my head down and wipe the table harder.

"If you ever want to make more than enough, you can talk to me." Keron speaks so softly I'm not sure I heard him correctly. "All I need is someone to go to San Fernando and bring a package up here for me. I'll give you a thousand for your first trip. It only goes up from there."

"Keron!" My father rarely yells and it takes me a while before I realise that it is he. "Is my son you talking to there."

Keron almost drops his Coke. "Sorry. Sorry, man. Sorry."

He almost cuts himself closing the switch blade. When my father walks over to me, Keron vanishes into the back.

"What he tell you?" my father asks.

"Nothing."

"Good." My father holds the big watch on his wrist up to my eyes. "Go on. And you have something to do? Go early. I paying you the same. Once you come back, eh?"

"Of course. Thank you."

Thank you!

★

I am far enough away from my hill that I can find a taxi.

"I'll take it by West Mall," I tell the driver.

"You'll take it before that," he throws back. When he stops by the flyover, I realise he has no intention of going further.

The starch I ironed into my shirt melts into flaccidity as I walk the rest of the way to the mall.

As I step inside, the blast of cold air chills the sweat on my face.

I hurry to the chrome and glass bathroom. In the mirror, I see a whitehead blossoming on the tip of my nose and squeeze it until the oil, bacteria and dead cells splatter. I wash my face, scrubbing my nose.

I imagine Ophelia's eyes – liquid-gold – looking at me over a cup of tea. She can't see me as I am – shirt spattered with sweat stains. The cigarette smoke from the bar clings to the creases in my clothes so that when I move, it's as if someone has just lit up. I soap my hands frantically, hoping that the smell will mask the lingering smokiness.

I breathe into my hand and the sour taste on my tongue tells me that my breath stinks. I'll order a cup of coffee as soon as I get there. The earthy smell will disguise it.

What if she wants to kiss my cheek first?

I pump liquid soap into my hand and slurp it from my palm. It coats my tongue with the flavour of chemicals. I gag and almost spit it out, but I force myself to swish it from cheek to cheek, folding the liquid under my tongue before I release the sticky salmon paste into the sink. I breathe into my hand again and inhale cheap chemicals. I inspect my shirt, which looked so crisp hanging on my door this morning.

If I get there early, I can position myself so that my left arm is across my body. That should block some of the worst sweat stains. Will I have to get up when she comes in?

OK. OK. Marcus, you're OK. You know what you're going to ask her: How was your morning? Learning your lines OK? Me too... I agree; it's the most challenging part of the play. But you would never think it from watching you on stage.

I cup my hands under the tap and drink some water. Each taste bud is screaming. I pull my comb out of my pocket and try to shape my curls. Unlike Ophelia's, they are too tight-knit.

I have never stolen before, but if only I knew how to get away with it, I would nab a Calvin Klein polo like the one Keron was wearing. Desperation makes you imagine yourself walking into Jardin in white cotton, more expensive than anything you've ever owned.

I check the time. I can't hide in the bathroom forever.

I weave through mothers and their children, couples holding hands and teenagers plugged into their iPods. I stop outside Jardin and look in.

Cupcakes, iced in crimson, tangerine and lime, stand in tiers under their glass casing. A waitress in a pink-and-white striped apron is slicing quiche Lorraine. My no-breakfast, no-lunch stomach clenches.

And then, Ophelia – sitting at a table for two in the far corner of the room.

Waiting.

She is wearing a cream dress with wide sleeves that flutter as she turns the page of her book. All the light is whisper-soft around her. Her edges blur and bleed like an impressionist painting. Her lips are the inside of a shell, pressing against one another as she reads – a self-kiss.

I want to ease a finger between them, part her mouth and touch her tongue. She does not look up. Takes it for granted, perhaps, that the world will look at her. Ophelia sits like her portrait is being painted – legs crossed lightly at the ankles, navel pulled towards her spine, shoulders fully spread.

How could I ever think I could walk in here and place myself in front of her?

I reach for my phone and tap in her number. My grandfather had a stroke. My mother had an asthma attack. I'm so sorry I can't make it.

Her phone rings.

Once.

Twice.

I'm standing where she cannot see me. I watch her hand disappear inside her purse and emerge with her phone. I'm so sorry.

"Ophelia…?"

★

I walk back to the bar, already spinning stories in my head. I see myself a thousand dollars richer, sauntering into Jardin in a rich-boy polo that is crisp and clean, and made of thick cotton that will soak up any sweat.

I apologise to Ophelia and tell her coffee is on me since I wasted her time.

I hope Keron is still at the bar.

THINGS WE DO NOT SAY

Bridgette's feet are killing her. The four-inch Jimmy Choos had seemed like a good idea when she'd ordered them online. Claret-coloured heels – just the right combination of classy and strappy. Shoes always make or break the outfit.

Now though, she feels as if the shoes have broken her feet. She's taken them off to drive home, but it still feels as if they're biting into her toes. She'll ask Eliot to rub her feet when she gets home. He's a meticulous masseur, his fingers always find her pressure points as if he knows what it's like to live in her skin.

Their third anniversary is coming up. Bridgette isn't sure what to get him; not just because he can afford almost anything he wants but also because he seldom seems to want anything at all. She's been toying with the idea of getting herself lacy black lingerie and dressing up for him, but that seems self-indulgent; isn't that more of a gift for her? She supposes she can get him another puzzle. The harder the better. He spends hours sorting the pieces into plastic containers of similar colours before fitting them together.

She's still thinking of it as she pulls into their garage. Maybe she can just ask him what he wants? He's never set much stock by surprises anyway.

She tosses her shoes aside as she enters the house. They are the only colour in their quartz and steel kitchen – it was once featured in an interior design special in *Caribbean Beat*. The photographer had showed up with a team to clean the kitchen before taking pictures. After a close inspection, the team admitted that the kitchen could not possibly be any neater than Eliot kept it. Bridgette makes a mental note to pick the shoes up before he does.

Eliot walks into the room. "What's the meaning of this?"

"Uh… I was going to pick them up," Bridgette says.

"Not that. This." He holds a book up to Bridgette. On the canary yellow cover, the words *Lusting After Love* are scrawled in orange.

"What is that?"

"A book of poems. It came in the mailbox."

"So?" She takes the book from Eliot. It's only then that she sees the author's name, written in a much smaller font: Dahlia Van Devender.

The pain in her feet spreads to her legs. She wants to sit down.

"Open it," Eliot says.

There is a table of contents. Some information on the publishers. And then the dedication: "For Bridgette, my burgundy bride".

Bridgette can't look at Eliot.

"I don't know what this means," she says.

"You don't?" Eliot's voice is excited. He has his chin in his hands like when he's thinking about the best place to start on a puzzle.

The last thing Bridgette wants is Eliot trying to solve the mystery of the book. She thinks of all the people he knows, the calls he can make.

"Firstly, this has to be a pen name," Eliot says. "Nobody is born with a name like that. Besides, I know all the Dutch families in Trinidad and there are no Van Devenders."

He tries to take the book back but she flings it away from them. She'd been aiming for the kitchen island but overshoots and it lands on the floor.

Eliot takes a step as if he is going to pick it up but then reconsiders.

"Look," Bridgette says, "I know Dahlia. I know she was writing a book but I had no idea that she was going to…" She glances at the book furtively.

"What does burgundy bride mean?"

"I have no idea."

"Why don't you ask her?"

"Sure."

Eliot takes another step towards the book. Bridgette can tell that he's not sure whether he should pick it up or not.

In an attempt to distract him, Bridgette says, "Those shoes weren't the best buy."

"No?" Eliot heads straight over to her shoes and picks them up. "What seems to be the problem?"

"They're too tight across the toes."

"Want me to take them to the shop in the mall to see if they can stretch them out?"

Eliot turns the shoes over in his hands.

"Yes please."

Bridgette strides over to the book, snatches it up and turns it face down on the countertop. Did he read it? She cannot imagine Eliot suffering through a book of poems. On the other hand, almost any man would feel compelled to read a book dedicated to his wife.

Maybe it hasn't occurred to him to read it? If so, she shouldn't plant the idea in his head by asking if he did.

"Did you… did you stop at the Arabic place for dinner?" Bridgette asks. That question somehow feels wrong.

"Yes," Eliot says. He drops the shoes into a plastic bag and ties the top. "Do you want mashed potatoes or rice?"

★

Bridgette and Eliot dated for seven uneventful years before he proposed. They rarely fought. If anything upset Bridgette, Eliot worked assiduously to make it better. If it was something he did, he promised not to do it again and, for the most part, he didn't. If it was something outside them, he figured out how to deal with it. A boss who put his hand on her thigh? One phone call and she had a new boss. An excruciating toothache that started throbbing at 2:00 pm on a Sunday? He knew a dentist who would love to open his office just for her.

Eliot himself never seemed to be upset by anything. Bridgette sometimes thought of him as someone who had learnt how to be human instead of being an actual human. He got by in most situations, but once in a while she had to help him out. When his mother died, the Ewing-Asquith family outdid themselves with fits of sobbing, paragraphs-long Facebook posts talking about what a good woman she was and orders for new, larger-than-life portraits of her to be hung in their houses.

Eliot was not sure what to do in the midst of this mêlée. Bridgette could tell that he was sorry but he didn't seem capable of feeling an emotion as extreme as grief.

Bridgette knew that his mother had been the type of woman who kept a stack of plastic cups just so the helper wouldn't drink out of her good glasses, and made the gardeners drink from the hose. The first time Bridgette had dinner with Eliot's family, Mrs Ewing-Asquith "forgot" to set a place for her and then asked Bridgette, at the table, whether her parents had ever taught her the proper way to hold a fork. Bridgette doubted that the heart-wrenching tributes pouring in for Eliot's mother (including an ass-kissing obituary published in *Catholic News*) were true. But she also knew that Eliot couldn't appear to seem callous.

So she helped him write the eulogy for his mother's funeral, where he described her as a role model who put family, friends and God before earthly things. (This was a lie so blatant Eliot had second thought about saying it, but Bridgette promised him that this was the sort of thing people said on such occasions.)

In bed that night Bridgette was thinking there was not a single instance in the last ten years when she'd seen Eliot sad or angry. If the death of his mother didn't do it, a thing like a book wouldn't either.

Although that depended on the contents of the book.

The bed murmurs as Eliot rolls onto his side. He likes to sleep facing her, with his head on his hand. Bridgette brushes away the hair that's fallen over his eyes. She leans over and kisses him on the cheek, feather-soft so that she won't wake him.

Then she slips out of bed and retrieves the book from the kitchen.

The Love that Dare Not Speak my name

You say it as if it has never been said before
"Dahlia"
Your words are petals on the floor

The hotel sheets fall
Off the hollows of your waist
Call after call
Goes unanswered

It's him – asking
When will you be
Back

But in the space we've made
We can sweep him aside
You may wear his ring but you are my
Burgundy bride

Flushed with the love
We rushed to make so that you could be
Home in time for dinner

In the morning, Bridgette calls the office and tells them there's a family emergency. Then she drives to Dahlia's apartment with scant regard for red lights. The bell isn't working so she slams the flat of her hand on the door. Whop. Whop. Whop.

"Who is it?" she hears Dahlia shouting from deep in the apartment.

Whop. Whop. Whop. Whop. Whop.

The door is wrenched open.

"Biddy," Dahlia says. The creases in her forehead vanish.

Bridgette stalks into the apartment and wallops the door shut.

"What the hell is wrong with you?"

She brandishes the book.

"Do you want Eliot to leave me?"

Bridgette forces the book open and bends the covers until they touch. "We can sweep him aside! You may wear his ring but you are my burgundy bride!" Her anger makes the words brittle.

"Biddy, I meant the poems to be a gift –"

Bridgette heaves the book past Dahlia. It hits the wall with a puff. Bridgette wishes it could have busted a hole through the wall.

"You just drop this *thing* in the mailbox? You meant for him to get it, didn't you? Is that it? You think you're in some sort of a competition with him?"

A smile twitches the edges of Dahlia's lips.

Bridgette slaps Dahlia across the face. She's never hit anyone before and the firmness of Dahlia's cheek surprises her.

Dahlia recoils like a comic book character. She's actually had to take several steps back.

"The dedication, that stupid dedication, that's bad enough. But to write a shitty poem that SPELLS IT OUT!"

Bridgette wants to hit Dahlia again. She wants to slam her and slam her as if she were the door.

There is a pain at the base of her throat that she's never felt before.

She can barely think of Eliot... of Eliot reading it, piecing it together like a puzzle.

"You know what your problem is?" Bridgette hisses. "You can never be happy with what you have – you always want more of everything."

As she says the words, she knows that this is exactly Dahlia's problem. She should have suspected something when Dahlia claimed to be a communist and started talking about the need to impose a maximum wage to prevent the creation of a one percent of super rich men (in Dahlia's explanation, women never cracked this glass ceiling). Dahlia's version of communism, thinks Bridgette, was all about getting more – more education, more job opportunities, more money – without having to do anything to earn it.

And now she's decided she wants more of Bridgette too.

"Biddy, I don't know if you've ever felt that the words inside you have to come out? There are times when I feel like I have to write about you –"

"Fine. But don't publish it."

"Biddy."

Even Dahlia's nickname for her is enraging.

Biddy! What a stupid, childish pet name.

Bridgette looks around for her purse, but she's never put it down. It's still hanging over her shoulder.

"Don't you dare call me," she says.

It takes everything she has not to bang the door behind her.

★

On the drive away from Dahlia, Bridgette interrogates her former self.

Why risk her relationship with Eliot, especially after they got married?

Why Dahlia?

Her old self tries to justify her choices. Hadn't she told Dahlia not to get too involved? Hadn't she said that she likes men too? That she loves Eliot?

Because she does. She loves him. And not because he's a man or he's rich or he's an Ewing-Asquith. At least, not just because of that.

Because he's more attentive to her than anyone she knows. Because he seems to have no expectations that she can't fulfil. Because he's constant, always the same Eliot.

Dahlia is someone who loves with words, with her body – even with that dreadful book of poems with its tacky yellow cover. But Eliot is someone who loves with deeds. When Bridgette had dengue fever, Eliot sat by their bed patiently immersing towels in ice-water before pressing them to her forehead and under her arms. The lecherous boss, the tooth-ache, the bank loan with 13% interest that her mother had taken out for carpel tunnel surgery – nothing was a problem when she was with Eliot.

Good sex is nice but it doesn't get a dentist to open his office on a Sunday.

Not that good sex can be a comfort now. Even the thought of it is tainted by the words of that poem.

Once she'd loved that Dahlia was passionate where Eliot was restrained. Impulsive where he was deliberate.

But where had that gotten her? With a stupid yellow book in their mailbox.

What could she tell Eliot if he asks about the book?

She feels frantic.

She goes through her catalogue of Eliot-memories. Is there anything she can say to convince him the book isn't important?

There's nothing.

Eliot had once explained to Bridgette that his childhood home abounded with unwritten rules. The bedroom bins were not for food. The outside bins were for "outside rubbish". The glass plates were for the family. The bone china plates were for his mother's friends. The frosted plates with gold patterns were for his father's guests. Eliot could play with the helper's children on the lawn but they were not allowed in the pool.

When his mother was visiting friends and the ironer came an hour early to see their father, Eliot was expected to keep his mouth shut. And even after the ironer was fired and denied access to the house, even when she stood crying at the gate because she said she was pregnant, Eliot was still forbidden to talk about it.

He'd nicknamed these rules *Things We Do Not Say* and one of his favourite things about being with Bridgette were that there were no such rules.

When he couldn't understand why she was so sad when her old dog died – on account of dogs usually living a relatively short life and her dog having lived for sixteen years – he asked her and she explained it to him and he nodded gravely. At the time, she'd felt proud because she'd known he could never have asked his mother this sort of thing.

And now? What can she say when he asks about the book?

Bridgette doesn't know where she is driving to. She pulls into the carpark of a bakery and sits still.

If she's honest, it hadn't even felt like cheating. She'd told herself that Eliot was unlike anyone she'd ever known. He probably wouldn't even feel upset if he found out.

She'd comforted herself with memories of their wedding planning when Eliot asked whether she wanted to include the church. He'd said that it was bad enough that a marriage might one day give lawyers access to their relationship but the thought that they should be obliged to make promises before an omniscient creator was excessive. He'd added that the thought that a god could care about whether two creatures slept only with each other for the rest of their lives was ridiculous. He'd begun a list of the things he would care about if he were a god, a very Eliot-like list that included things like the environment and whether every person on earth had their basic needs met.

Back then, Bridgette had saved that conversation mentally in case she needed it. If a god didn't care about monogamy, surely Eliot wouldn't.

But now?

She's just like his father fucking the ironer when his mother was away.

A tawdry, dirty person who doesn't deserve him.

Bridgette realises she is crying. She checks her purse for tissues. Her glove compartment. Eventually, she blows her nose in her sleeve.

★

Amazon delivers a Chopard watch for their anniversary. A book on climate science and conservation. A 6000-piece puzzle of Venice at sunset – they went to Italy on their honeymoon. Bridgette buys a lacy black teddy and a thong. She gets a local chocolate house to make a box especially for Eliot. They send it with his name engraved on the cover.

She wraps everything in the most expensive paper she can buy. Every present gets a bow.

She waits for him to ask. What happened to the book?

Instead, he asks where she wants to go for their anniversary dinner.

She wants whatever he wants.

Once, their house phone rings and she races to it.

Surely Dahlia wouldn't call here? Or would she do it now that Bridgette has literally thrown her book away?

It turns out to be a telemarketer.

It takes her three tries to put the phone back in the dock.

Bridgette decides she has to make Dahlia promise never to talk to Eliot.

She dials Dahlia's number. She feels a twinge of the old excitement in her belly. She hates that she feels it.

"Biddy?" Dahlia demands. The other woman sounds breathless.

"Can I see you?" Bridgette asks.

★

She's puts on the stretched-out Jimmy Choos with a black sweater dress. She texts Eliot saying that she has to help her mother with something.

On the drive to Dahlia's, she starts thinking of a speech.

You're someone I've always admired.

That part is true. Dahlia is obsessed with living her truth. She was born Chenelle Chapman and then changed her name to reflect the woman she was becoming. She marched in Trinidad's first Gay Pride parade.

And I know you think I'm a sellout.

Dahlia hates Bridgette's pink diamond engagement ring because it is an emblem of the triumph of late-stage capitalism over Bridgette's identity.

And I know you think I don't love Eliot.

But I do. I do. These days have taught me that I love him to the point of pain.

But I…

But Bridgette has no more speech. What is she really saying? Thank you for showing me how much I need my husband. Please never call me again. And if you can ask your publishers to pull your book off shelves, then even better.

She knows what Dahlia is like when she's angry. None of this mumbo-jumbo will do.

Almost without thinking, she's parking at the side of the road (Dahlia's apartment complex has no guest parking spots).

She sits in the car and tries to think of what she can say.

I know I'm selfish. But please don't ruin my happiness.

There is a loud bang and Bridgette jumps. This part of Diamond Vale is starting to see more shootings. But no, it's just a man closing his car trunk.

She steps out of the car and looks in the mirror. "Bridgette Ewing-Asquith," she says aloud, "you can do this thing."

Dahlia lets her in on the first knock. She looks like she hasn't threaded her eyebrows in weeks. Bridgette inhales the sweaty scalp smell of un-shampooed hair.

"Do you want to sit?" Dahlia asks. Her tone is unlike any Bridgette has heard from her. It is flat as if there are no inflections to words.

Bridgette smooths the front of her dress. "Yes please," she says.

There are three small stacks of *Lusting After Love* on the living room table. Bridgette sits as far away from them as possible.

Dahlia sits, clasps her hands together. Bridgette sees the veins in the back of her hand rise.

Bridgette clears her throat. "You're someone I've always admired. And I know you think I'm a sellout."

"Sellout?" Dahlia asks. "You have to believe in something to sellout."

"I do believe in something," Bridgette says, louder than she intended.

"Of course," Dahlia says. She points at Bridgette's shoes. "You believe in things."

"I love Eliot," Bridgette says.

"So then why did you?"

"Because I never thought he would find out."

"That's it?"

"That's it."

"Well thank you for your time," Dahlia says. "And I'm sorry about the book. It is all so clear to me now. How could I dare to have feelings about you? Shouldn't I have known I'm just the side piece? Naughty Dahlia, for getting out of line." And Dahlia whacks herself across the cheek.

Bridgette jumps up. "Please don't do that."

"Now it bothers you?"

"I'm very sorry," Bridgette says. "I shouldn't have hit you before. And I shouldn't... I shouldn't have done what I did."

"I assume I'm the "what" that you did, since you clearly don't regret Eliot."

But Dahlia is cracking. She could never maintain the ice queen routine for too long.

She cries two greasy tears.

Bridgette wants to hug her.

"I know I'm selfish," she says.

That makes Dahlia start sobbing in earnest.

★

Bridgette feels the weight of her awfulness on the drive back home. What had Eliot and Dahlia seen in her?

And who was better off now? Eliot with her? Dahlia without her?

The question is stupid. Eliot is better off. He's always been.

As she lets herself in, she feels relief to be back in the quiet order of their house and the smooth, straight lines of their kitchen. The countertops gleam even brighter than usual. She pictures Eliot's fastidious polishing.

The roses on the kitchen counter are a shocking ruby. She couldn't have missed their anniversary? But no, that's not until November ninth.

She sees something beside the flowers. It is a yellow book with orange writing on the cover.

The edge of a white envelope peeks out from beneath the book. Bridgette tears it open and recognises the precisely spaced letters of Eliot's handwriting.

Things We Do Not Say

Does writing like
this
make me a poet?

It's very hard to rhyme

Bridgette
I know there are things we're not supposed to say

But I know
And I don't love you any less

And if you want we can talk about it in the morning
Or we can never talk about it at all

Love always,
Eliot

THE COURSE

He's always had thirsty skin. Sitting in the rain, washing off the dirt from last night's exploits, he lets his pores drink.

The air is streaked with thunder.

He's spent the earliest part of the morning retching up a chunky concoction brindled with blood. Tendrils of wispy hair have wrapped themselves around his fingers. There is no way hair like that could have belonged to an adult.

A child he thinks, feeling sicker. He doesn't know for sure, though. He can never remember.

Looking through the rain, he sees Coraline's face behind the window. Her terracotta curls swirl around her head in an early-morning mess.

When the clouds have bled themselves dry, Coraline picks her way through the puddles.

"It happened again last night," she tells him.

"I know it happened."

"It". It is the thing neither of them knows. They tried to medicate "it" with doctors' visits, sleeping pills and hypnosis. But it still leaves their doors hanging off hinges, scratched as if a giant wolf were trying to get out. It leaves Coraline to wake up to his torn clothes and an empty house. There is a local word for men who turn into monsters – lagahoo – but they have come to an unspoken agreement to never say the word aloud – after all, neither he nor she has ever witnessed it.

"You remember it?" she asks.

He hates the high, hopeful sound of her voice, almost making him wish he could remember.

"No. But I've been throwing up all morning."

The first filaments of sunlight find their way through the clouds.

"Mrs Cooper called this morning," Coraline says. "She asked if we saw her daughter."

He barely has time to lean forward before the sludge bursts from his lips. His throat convulses with wave after wave, and even when his stomach is empty, he keeps heaving.

Coraline has somehow sidestepped the vomit.

"Cora, you must know that I–I would never…"

"I know," she says gently. She stoops down and runs her fingers through his hair. "Still. I've been researching what we could do about it."

"Researching?"

"Of course," she says. "I think there are alternative channels we can use. Maybe visit a non-traditional doctor."

"Non-traditional doctor? You mean obeah?"

She brings her teeth to her lower lip and chews – as if tasting the word. "Yes, obeah," she says eventually.

Where would he – or she – find a practitioner? The thought of Coraline asking around for someone who dabbles in the occult is ridiculous.

"I Googled it," she says, as if he'd spoken aloud. And, seeing his face, she continues, "They're businesspeople like anyone else. They need to advertise their services."

He isn't sure he can trust an obeah man who advertises online. What would an obeah man do? Pay for a Facebook ad?

He wants to say that this sounds absurd – but isn't his whole life an absurdity? Why not? Now that they've discussed it, he's amazed that they haven't tried it sooner.

She holds a slim arm out and helps him to his feet. He wipes the last of the bile from around his mouth. "I suppose we could give it a shot," he says.

★

The road to the Northern Range was chiselled into the edge of the mountain long ago. Their car winds through its curves. To their right the precipice gapes green; trees have clawed their way up the steep rock face and are growing where he would not have thought anything could grow.

"So you really found this man on Google?"

"It's a woman," Coraline says.

In the car, a string quartet is playing Michael Jackson's "Human Nature". Coraline is the only person he knows who listens to this kind of music. He doesn't know enough about music to be able to hear the instruments speak to each other like she does. When they first started dating, she would say things like, "Listen to the first violin", but she'd stopped that – maybe because she didn't want him to feel as if she were lording her upbringing over him. She'd been born to parents who played classical music at dinner and who discussed, in dead seriousness, whether Shakespeare was more of a comic or tragic genius.

"Do you know what I'm thinking?" Coraline asks.

He imagines that she's thinking that if she were in love with another man she wouldn't have to go through this.

"No," he says.

"I was thinking that if this works – if you get better – maybe we can talk about having a baby."

A flock of parrots rises from the canopy in a fury of flapping.

He can't believe it. A baby? How could she even put such a thought into words?

More than that, Coraline has never been the type to want traditional things. Wasn't that part of the reason she'd asked him out? Wasn't that the reason why, after years of dating, she'd told him that she didn't believe in marriage?

Suddenly, he is aware that the car is very small and cold and, even if he wanted to get out, there is nothing but trees around them. There seem to be no words to capture the monstrosity of his aversion. Coraline turned thirty last month. Is this some sort of feminine thing, where she's worried that her woman's clock is ticking her baby-making years away?

"Cora…" he says, trusting that she will hear the meaning in his voice, as she does with the violins.

"I mean, we wouldn't do it until we're sure that you're better," she says. Only her hands betray her – the knuckles squeezing the steering wheel are bright red.

"Is this something you really want?" he asks.

"Yes. Look, I know why you're worried. But you would never hurt our baby. I know it."

How can she know it? When they started living together, she'd thought he sometimes went to the bar down the road at night. He'd told her the truth – he couldn't really remember those nights. But he'd never told her about the disfigured shreds of human bodies that he woke up with. Skin under his fingernails. A mangled earlobe clutched in his palm. Hair wrapped around his fingers. Somehow, she'd connected clues he wasn't aware of leaving. And even then, she hadn't left. Was it because she loved him? But why would someone like her love someone like him at all, let alone enough to stay?

He thinks of Mrs Cooper's daughter. A few months after she was born, Mrs Cooper pushed her around in a pink pram, showing her off to the neighbourhood. He remembers the awful smallness of the baby's hands. How could hands that feeble do anything? He'd taken the baby's foot in his own large hand and marvelled that a whole human foot could nestle so snugly in his palm.

No. No. Best not to think about it.

The deepest string instrument is groaning. Is it the viola or the cello? He's not sure.

Coraline turns up a steep road – the car is almost vertical and he wonders whether they can manage this ascent. Her lips are mashed into one another, as if she can drag the car up by

willpower alone. All around them is green. The car keeps
climbing until they've reached what is, apparently, the end of the
road. Coraline reverses into a minuscule space between a mora
tree and a yellow poui. If she is afraid, she doesn't show it.

"There's nothing here," he says, and he's surprised to feel
relief.

"This is the place," Coraline insists. She gets out of the car
and looks around.

He gets out too. "What are we looking for?"

Coraline doesn't answer, she just keeps combing through
the trees with her eyes. "There!" She is pointing to a thin dirt
track that leads further into the forest. She walks over and loops
her arm through his. He leans into the warmth of her and
almost tells her that they should go back, but she is already
pulling him onto the path.

The walk through the trees is long and slow. To him, it feels
as if they are going nowhere. Coraline lifts his hand to her lips
and kisses the tips of his fingers. "Don't worry about what I said
in the car – about the baby."

Abruptly, their eyes are assaulted by the relentless turquoise
of the Caribbean Sea. The earth falls away and, miles below,
they see the white froth of the waves rolling into the shore. "It's
beautiful," Coraline breathes.

Beautiful isn't the word he would use – it's too sudden, this
absence of land. He would like a hill that slopes sweetly to a
white sand shore, not the viciousness of this drop or the
barbaric yellow of the beach below.

"Are you two enjoying the view?"

He jumps.

Coraline presses her hand into the small of his back. "We
are, thank you very much."

If he can avoid turning around, maybe he can ignore that
there is another person here with them. Maybe he can just
pretend that they're taking a Sunday drive through the North-

ern Range and they've stopped to sightsee. Coraline pivots and he is forced to face the speaker. There is nothing terrible about the woman in front of them; in fact, her face seems to be a composite of many women he's met before.

"I'm Coraline." She holds out her hand as if this is a business meeting.

The woman shakes her hand. "Edith," she says.

Edith. It's the name of an old lady who should be baking cookies for grandchildren.

"Thank you for agreeing to see us," Coraline says. "It's hard to explain. But he…"

"Oh yes," Edith says, "it's screaming out of his skin."

She walks up to him and takes his head in her hands. Her eyes drill into his – her pupils are horribly dilated, a mass of blackness almost the size of a coin. His scalp starts to burn under her fingers.

She lets him go. "Only ever at night?" she asks.

"Yes."

Edith nods. "That's when the shadow is strongest."

"You know what it is? What is it?" Coraline asks.

Edith turns to look at her. "There are some things you do not name."

He can see that Coraline wants to ask why.

"To name something is to give it more power," Edith says. "And if you call a name, you never know what might answer."

Edith spreads her arms wide. Only then does he notice that the parrots are not shrieking. Even the waves seem subdued. He has the awful feeling that they are listening.

"It won't be easy to overcome," Edith says. "And you won't be the same afterwards – it will be like tearing yourself apart."

"We'll do whatever it takes!" Coraline says.

"Will you do whatever it takes?" Edith asks him.

He thinks of Coraline who poured six years of her life into him. She's given up so much. "I will," he says. It feels like a wedding vow.

Edith nods. "For the next three nights, don't sleep. Not even a wink. You need to starve this thing before you can start the course."

"Course?" Coraline asks. "Like a course of antibiotics?"

"A lot like that," Edith says. She reaches out and grabs his hands. "If you stop the course," she says, "it would be better never to have started at all."

"I understand."

"And you can pay," Edith says.

★

He plumps a pillow for her in their bedroom.

"You can sleep," he tells Coraline.

She shakes her head. "Who will keep you up if you start nodding off?"

"But you have work tomorrow."

"Daddy can write me a sick note," she says. He tries not to think of her doctor father, who always looks at him as if he is a disease to be treated.

Coraline crawls across the bed until she is sitting opposite him. In the darkness, she leans forward and presses her forehead to his. "Imagine," she says, "Everything can be totally normal. We won't have to move any more. We can pick a place we like; buy a house."

He hopes that she will not mention a baby again. Maybe to prevent her doing that, he kisses her. Coraline always sighs when his lips part hers. She threads her fingers together behind his neck and pulls herself on top of him. She says, "I suppose this is one way to stay awake."

★

On the third night, he feels the weight of sleeplessness behind his eyelids. Although he's been drinking water, his lips are cracked and dry.

He insists that she sleeps. "How will you drive back there if you're exhausted?" he asks.

Coraline is unsure. "What if you nod off?"

"I won't."

This isn't good enough for her. He can see Coraline thinking. "I know! Why don't you stand in the shower?"

"For the whole night?"

"You can take a chair and sit in there," she suggests.

Why not? He gets one of the cheap plastic chairs that they use to sit in the garden and lets the cold water sluice off him. "Don't close your eyes," Coraline warns. "Not even for a second."

"I promise."

Alone, he thinks of Mrs Cooper's daughter. There are electronic signs scattered throughout the country to help the Anti-Kidnapping Squad locate missing people. Large letters read HELP FIND ME; below there's a picture of the person who can't be found and numbers that those with tips can call. He's always found these pictures to be tragic – the person in the picture is often smiling. To think that person used to be so happy and now they're kidnapped. Or worse.

Pictures of Mrs Cooper's daughter have started to appear on the signs. HELP FIND ME. He can't bear to look at the girl's chubby cheeks and wide-mouthed smile.

He isn't just doing this for Coraline. He's doing this for Mrs Cooper's daughter and for anyone else who may have come before.

He realises that he is relaxed in the shower – his skin is happy to be bathed so generously.

He dreams he's sitting in an enormous shadow. Or is it his shadow, swollen to monstrous proportions?

The water spatters into his open mouth.

How could he be dreaming if he were never asleep?

He looks around as if expecting to see the shadow pooling around him but there is only his own, a blob beneath his feet.

★

There is no violin music for their drive back into the Northern Range. Coraline is worried that it may put him to sleep. Instead they're listening to music where cymbals clash and something that sounds like cannon fire thunders at regular intervals.

"Maybe we could ask my mother to help us find a house," Coraline says.

He wishes she weren't so hopeful. He wonders how disappointed she will be if it doesn't work.

The car groans as Coraline forces it up that near-vertical inclination. The headache that has been banging around in his skull intensifies. But he knows that he can't suggest going back.

As they walk the path through the trees, he notices that it seems darker than before. Did the trees always shield the sunlight like this?

He reaches for Coraline's hand and is reassured by the feel of her fingers interwoven with his.

"Did you sleep?"

Goose pimples rise on his skin.

He swivels to see Edith waiting for them. Her head is wrapped in a brilliantly white cloth. It is the only speck of brightness in this place.

"Did you sleep?" she asks again.

"No."

She stares. And he almost tells her that he isn't sure. But he thinks of Coraline, who needs him to be better.

"I didn't," he says.

Coraline squeezes his hand.

Edith picks a wooden box off the floor. It's filled with glass bottles, each a different colour and shape. Surely the colours can't matter. He's forced to confront the possibility that this is nothing more than showmanship and after all this money and effort, nothing will have changed.

"This is your last chance to tell me anything you need to," Edith says.

He remains silent.

She nods. "Drink one a day after the moon comes up. Start with the shortest bottle and end with the tallest."

Edith squares her shoulders and looks from Coraline to him. "You cannot stop the course. No matter the side effects."

"Side effects?" Coraline asks.

"Of course. Something like this – you think it's going to go quietly?" Edith asks.

Coraline lets his hand go and stands between him and Edith. "What can we expect?"

"I'm not asked to do this kind of thing a lot," Edith says. "Let's just say that he may feel unwell."

He can see the possibilities bouncing around in Coraline's head. "How often have you done this before?" she asks.

"Once."

The air around them is wet and heavy with mist.

He looks at Coraline's face and he loves the determined line of her mouth, as if she can make this happen by wanting it enough.

"Am I allowed to sleep?" he asks Edith.

"If you can manage it."

He feels so exhausted he doubts that there is any potion that can stop him from sleeping.

"Begin tonight," Edith tells them.

Coraline draws a fat envelope from her purse and hands it over.

★

That night, he pours Coraline a glass of wine. They've stored the wooden box in the coolest, driest corner of their kitchen. He runs his fingers along the glossy glass of the bottles. He finds the shortest bottle and uncorks it. It is a brilliant orange.

"Do you think the colour matters?" he asks Coraline.

"I doubt it."

They clink the glasses together and drink. His throat is rigid, waiting for the worst but there is no flavour. The liquid is syrupy and thick but it tastes like coconut water.

Coraline's fingers are locked around the stem of the wine glass. He worries that she'll snap it if she keeps clutching it like that.

"How do you feel?" she asks.

"Fine."

He doesn't want to admit that he's doubting whether anything will change. Instead, he slips the glass from her fingers, wraps his arms around her narrow shoulders and rests his head on hers.

She squeezes him ferociously. He hasn't ever felt this iron embrace from her before. How has he missed her desperation? Has he become so wrapped up in himself that he's only thought of her as someone who cares for him? Someone better connected, who always makes a call when they need to get out of a neighbourhood quickly.

Coraline loosens her grip and looks at him. "Nothing?"

"I feel a bit queasy." This is a lie, but he says it because he wants her to think it's working.

She nods. "Let me know if it gets any worse."

★

On the third day, he still hasn't felt any differently. There are seven vials and he suspects that the whole thing is a hoax. Coraline constantly feels his forehead for a fever. She's even brought a bowl to the bedside in case he throws up. He hasn't had the courage to tell her that he feels exactly as he always has, so he's invented a series of minor aches and pains.

On this night, Coraline pours herself more wine than usual. He pulls the third vial out of the box. It's an aggressive azure, like the sky on a blistering day.

"To us," Coraline says, as she touches her glass to his.

He drinks it all.

She is looking at him with her head tilted to one side.

"What's wrong?" he asks.

She blinks and her mouth moves. Is she speaking?

Did he hear himself when he spoke just now?

"Cora?"

He knows he said her name but he hears nothing.

He claws at his ears. What the hell?

"Cora?" He wonders whether he's screaming.

Her lips are moving but there is silence. The total absence of sound is a horror. Surely this will end? Edith would have told him if the potions were going to make him live in a soundless world.

Coraline's hands are on his cheeks. He sees them but he feels nothing.

He grabs her arms but there is no texture to her skin.

He looks at her – focusing on the thing that first made him love her, her wide eyes. He sees her emerald irises stretching bigger than he's known them; he sees the whites of her eyes streaked with red.

"Cora?"

Sweat bursts from his pores in a paroxysm of feeling. He is convulsed with tremors. He doubles over, digging his fingers into Coraline's hips. He feels as if a fist has grabbed his oesophagus. Even as he drops to his knees, he welcomes the unforgiving hardness of their kitchen tiles.

"… hear me now?" Coraline's voice touches him like a kiss.

"Yes." His teeth are chattering so violently that he can barely say the word.

Even the air seems to be stinging his eyes. The tears burn as they roll down his face; his skin screeches.

He doesn't know how long he kneels there savouring the return to sensation. He feels her fingers soft on his arm. She clutches his hand and pulls him to his feet. He staggers, lumbering into her so that they crash into the fridge. He wants to ask if he's hurt her but there is no way he can speak.

She forces his arm over her shoulder and guides him to the bedroom.

He collapses onto the bed. She steps away and he reaches out to her. He tries to talk but spit dribbles out of his mouth and all he can taste is salt.

He must tell her – he never meant to push her. He wants to see if she's been bruised from being shoved against the fridge.

She covers her mouth with a hand, but although she drops her chin, she never turns away. Even after one of his nights, when he'd awoken with no memory of what he'd done, she'd never been afraid to meet his gaze.

Is she afraid now? Is he frothing at the mouth? Is that what this spit is?

He grunts – the closest he can come to words. Her eyes meet his and it's not fear he sees. It's pity.

★

"You have to drink it."

He will sooner die than drink the fourth bottle. He reaches out to push Coraline away.

His sweat has soaked through the sheet and is beginning to saturate the mattress.

No. He wants to go back. Nothing can be worth this.

"Please!"

His neck groans with pain as he turns his head to look at Coraline.

"Please!"

She presses her palm to his chest. Even her touch is torture. He jerks away.

"Please. We're doing this for our future. For the baby. You don't know this but I stay up at night and think about names." Coraline's voice cracks. "I know you'd be the best daddy."

Daddy?

"Please."

She pushes two fingers between his teeth and forces his lips apart. He imagines biting her – anything to prevent this. She raises the glass to his mouth and pours the liquid in. It sears his tongue and it takes every shred of willpower to release the muscles in his throat so that he can swallow.

He doesn't know what he can do to get relief. He hadn't imagined that a person could hurt like this.

★

He dreams. Coraline appears to him in a myriad of incarnations. A ribbon around his ribs. A hand up under his heart. A bow pulled across a violin.

"What do you want most?" Coraline asks him.

He wants her. He wants love. He tries to tell her but his throat burns and the words rise and drift away like steam.

★

The whole world is agony. Had he ever missed hearing? Each noise now is a nail in his eardrum. Had he ever wanted to feel? He's torn his shirt off because the fabric was fire on his skin.

Coraline appears with another bottle. He drinks the pain.

Another bottle. How much time has passed? He can't track it. He can't track anything.

Let me die.

Anything would be better. Anything at all.

He realises that he is swallowed by the shadow. It devours everything he touches – everything he's touched. It wraps Coraline in its darkness. It pours into the many-coloured bottles they've stored in the kitchen.

When he wakes up, the sweat on his skin is cold. The pain is a rawness in his throat. A hollowness in his stomach. But the bone-shattering shaking has stopped.

"Cora?" He can't believe his mouth had found the word.

The door bursts open and she flies inside. They look at each other. He has no idea what she is seeing.

He realises that the thing sticking his thighs together is urine. He tries to sit up but is too weak.

"Are you hungry?" she asks.

"Starved."

After eating almost everything they have in the house, he showers. Coraline strips the sheets from the mattress and soaks it with shampoo.

He slips coming out of the shower and bangs his elbow against the wall.

In the mirror, he sees his ribs push out against his stomach like inverted wings. How long has he gone without eating? Is the course over?

Coraline is standing in the doorway with fresh boxers and a T-shirt. Her eyes rove over his body, pausing on the protruding ribs and his jutting thighbones. He wants her to look away. He gestures for the boxers and she stoops and helps him step into them as if he were a child.

He bends forward and they put on the T-shirt together.

"Today is the seventh day," Coraline says. She squeezes his hand. He winces and her hold relaxes.

Her eyes are lustrous. Now that the pain has subsided so that he can think, he allows himself to imagine – for the first time – a baby with her corkscrew curls and his copper skin.

"Do you think you can make it to the kitchen?"

"Of course."

But he has to lean on her to get there.

She pops a bottle of champagne and it hisses as she fills her flute.

He opens the wooden box and is confronted with the last ruby bottle.

It is surprisingly light. He uncorks it and peers inside. Is there anything in there?

It couldn't be empty.

"To endings," Coraline chirps, clinking her glass on his.

He tips the bottle upside down. A single droplet falls onto his tongue. It sizzles before slipping down his throat.

Is that it? Was there supposed to be more?

"What's wrong?" Coraline asks.

"There was only one drop."

She frowns. "But you drank it?"

"Yes."

Coraline's lips are compressed as she contemplates it. "No one could have interfered with those bottles," she declares. "That's probably how it's supposed to be."

He wishes he could feel so sure.

"Don't worry so much," Coraline says. But her voice is saturated with doubt.

He remembers, as if seeing it through a haze, Coraline's confidence when she'd insisted that they visit an obeah woman. Where is the confidence now that the deed's been done?

"Is the bed dry?" he asks.

"I don't think so," she says. "I've been sleeping on the couch."

They pad to the living room and fit themselves awkwardly on the couch. He is sandwiched between her and the oppressive softness of the cushions.

Their curtains cut the moonlight out of the room.

Coraline shifts against him and then turns so that her face is buried in his chest.

She presses her lips just above his nipple. It's over," she says. "We just need time to realise that we can start a normal life."

He buries his nose in her hair and breathes the hibiscus scent of her shampoo. Although it makes his wrists hurt, he runs his hands in gentle lines across her back.

He feels her shoulders relax as she nuzzles into his chest.

"I love you."

★

He wakes up naked. Blades of grass are piercing the back of his neck. He lifts his eyelids to see the impenetrable greyness of the sky. His eyes adjust and he sees the myriad of mahogany trees that surround their backyard.

Something sloshes inside his stomach.

The vomit shoots out of his mouth and splatters on his face. He rolls onto his hip and his throat expels brown lumps slicked in blood.

What is that? It looks like an earlobe.

He retches again.

Lightning explodes across the sky and he waits for the thunder. It feels as if the rumble starts in the marrow of his bones.

He pushes himself to his knees and his eyes turn to the windows but Coraline isn't standing behind them.

He walks to the back of their house. The door is wide open. It isn't like Coraline to leave it unlocked. He steps in listening for any sounds from inside.

The kitchen is a tangle of steel, wood and glass. The husk of the microwave seems to have been hurled against the wall. The fridge door is torn off and the hinges hang uselessly off its edge.

Who could have done this?

He looks down at his hands. Red curls are knotted around his fingers.

"Coraline!" His voice ricochets off the walls and bounces back into him. "Cora!" His feet fly out of the kitchen and into the living room. The couch has been turned over and ripped to shreds. Tiles are cracked. Nails appear to have scraped the paint off the walls. Splotches of something violet stain the floor.

He shakes his head.

No.

He races to the bedroom. The mattress lies uncovered. Coraline's phone is lying on the nightstand. He tries to turn it on but it's dead.

He plugs it in and then plunges in and out of each room.

All around him is emptiness and watery light streaming through the windows.

He returns to the bedroom and turns the phone on. The date and time stare at him.

Impossible. All that time couldn't have passed.

The phone vibrates. 59 missed calls. 10 Voicemail messages. 66 text messages.

He closes his eyes and presses Coraline's phone to him.

"I wouldn't," he says.

He remembers the day they started the course, Coraline had asked Edith if she'd done this before.

"Once," Edith said.

They'd never asked her if it had worked.

PRESENT

The sunlight makes the ocean golden. The younger me would have stripped to her panties and run down to the waves. I would have felt the sea buoy me, raise my hips like a lover before laying me down on the bed. I would have turned up my chin to the sky to be baptised by the sun. I would have spread my arms like a four-pointed starfish bridging worlds.

But the new me – the me I have become – sits in the shade. Her scar burns under the concentrated beam of sunlight, the skin reddening around the puckered scar till it looks bloodied and raw. She recalls the day she first received the wound – one of many mementos of what she had once believed was love.

A quietness has descended over the beach, like a shroud. Ants are black freckles on the sand, tearing a crab apart. They will strip everything that made the crab a crab and leave only an empty shell.

★

I creep into our house like a burglar. In our living room, the portrait of Michael looms over me. The photograph was taken twenty years ago. The hairstyle is the one he wore to the day he died. The room is a monument to his illustrious family. There is his mother in her wedding dress – a famous Brazilian beauty who moved to Trinidad for the love of his father – or so they said. There is his father, one of the many Clapham doctors who corrected anyone who made the mistake of calling him "Mister"; and there is his grandfather, a black-and-white version of his grandson.

What is stopping me from pulling all these Claphams off our walls – *my* walls?

I'll begin with Michael. "Well, Dr Clapham, I hope you don't mind being wrapped in brown paper and laid face down in a cupboard for eternity."

When I first met Michael, he had just become Dr Clapham. My father needed a hip replacement and I couldn't believe that this young man in the white coat was competent enough to do it.

Michael had seen my doubt. "I can stitch your dress from neck to hem and the line will be perfect," he'd said. "And I'll stitch your father up just as well."

And he had pierced the neck of my dress with a long silver needle to make his point.

At our wedding, he'd told the story to the whoops of our guests and the applause of my father.

He didn't say that the needle had pricked my skin, sharp and sudden, but not enough – then – to draw blood.

The jangling of my phone makes me jump. The ladder I'd gotten out of the cupboard clatters to the floor.

Only Ashley. "Hello, love," I say.

"Hey, Mum. How are you feeling today?"

"Not too bad."

"Just checking to see if you want Chinese for dinner," she says.

"Sweetheart, it's OK."

"Come on, I bet you haven't had a proper meal since breakfast."

Since Michael's death, Ashley's come to see me almost every day.

"Maybe just some steamed wontons," I say.

What will she think of me removing her father's picture?

Ashley and I had been relegated to the row of photographs immediately below Michael's parents.

Being a plain woman, I take an inordinate pride in knowing that my daughter is a great beauty. I look at Ashley's picture, taken when she graduated from medical school. Her hair is just as black as her university gown and it falls in feathery layers along her egret neck. Her hazel eyes, which I call "owl eyes", shine big and bright. I've seen her boiling with fever, with the blood risen just below her skin, and I've seen her under-eyes sagging with lack of sleep when she was studying late. Even then she never lost that Ashley lustre.

I've always considered it a private victory that, although she looks so much like Michael, her personality is nothing like his.

I lift the ladder back to the storage cupboard. I have to tilt it sideways and the effort leaves a dull ache in my lower back. Michael always told me to sit up straighter, or I would have back problems in my later years.

I potter around, then wash the single teacup in the sink. I hear Ashley's keys in the lock before she sweeps into the kitchen. Her perfume – white gardenia – settles over the room.

She kisses me, then produces a series of Styrofoam bowls. "I got a little extra just in case you felt for something else."

Char siu pork, white flesh steaming. Black mushrooms sprinkled with chives. Sweet-and-sour shrimp coated in sticky sauce. Her father had been allergic to shellfish, which meant there was never any shrimp in our house.

"I'll start with the wontons," I say. "You really shouldn't have spent so much money."

She rolls her eyes. "I think my budget can handle it."

It's true – none of the Clapham doctors has ever wanted for money.

Ashley ladles food into a plate.

"What's that on your finger?" I demand.

Ashley glances at her ring finger, as if surprised to see the diamond there.

"Oh Mum. I am so sorry. We literally got engaged the night

before Daddy passed. And I didn't think it was in good taste to wear the ring so soon after, but I do put it on when we're alone and I guess I forgot to take it off. I wanted to sit you down and tell you properly."

Ashley takes a step forward and extends her arms.

I think of her boyfriend. Anthony Le Blanc. Another tall, arrogant surgeon like Michael with a meticulous hairstyle, and a way of saying his family's last name as if expecting you to know his father, his father's father, and the illustrious history of his extended French Creole family, who have graced our island for over two hundred years.

"Oh, Ashley, no." I hadn't meant to say it. But the thought of my beautiful daughter giving up her freedom and her own apartment with a view of the Savannah to be the wife of Anthony Le Blanc feels like a needle piercing my neck.

People talk about the wonderful paediatrician she is and her special way with their children. No one ever spoke about her father with such fondness. Now she'll have to give that up to host dinner parties and attend functions as Mrs Anthony Le Blanc.

Yes, they say you can keep your career. But when the baby comes, you can't expect them to lose sleep at night when they have an important surgery in the morning. And even before a baby, when they must come home to a hot meal, you have to be the one at home to prepare it. Can't be store-bought. Can't be leftovers. What kind of wife reheats lasagne?

Men like Michael Clapham and Anthony Le Blanc: their mothers would walk over a bed of nails to bring them a glass of ice water when they were thirsty. And they expect their wives to be like their mothers – little by little, day by day, their husbands become their whole life.

"Are you crying?" Ashley asks.

"Yes," I say.

"Mum, don't worry. This doesn't mean I won't have time for you, especially with Daddy gone."

I shake my head. This isn't about me; it is about my daughter throwing away her future to be a wife.

My skin feels paper-thin as I wipe the tears away. Ashley's hand, weighed down with that gaudy rock, lifts a napkin to my cheeks. I take it, still not wanting to look at her ring.

Can anything I say make her reconsider? I only know that I will be very sorry if I don't try.

"Ashley, it's not about me. But you... and Anthony?... Marriage is a serious commitment... and if you have children –"

"Anthony and I have talked about children." She brings a hand to her abdomen.

She can't be pregnant. Not my daughter swollen with another Anthony Le Blanc growing fat inside her.

If she is, it will be too late to sit her down and talk to her about motherhood. I'm already thinking of what I should say instead. How about "This is the greatest gift you can give your husband"? My own mother had told me that when I was pregnant with Ashley. She'd been so excited to be a grandmother.

But I can't say anything.

Ashley looks down and I feel as if a rock has been dropped into my stomach.

"The thing is..." she says, "Anthony wanted children but I never really felt the need to be a mother. I know, I work with children all the time. But that's what children are to me: work. Anthony's such a feminist, he respects that women have choice, but it took a while for him to come to terms with the no-children thing. He even said he could be a stay-at-home dad. But honestly, I can't imagine him changing diapers and running after kids all day. And I would still have to push them out! Sorry for being so graphic."

Ashley tries to look at me but her eyes move back to the floor.

"Anyway, our conversations made Anthony think a lot about why he used to say he wanted kids. Was it a result of social expectations or did he really want them? I know I should have talked to you sooner, but I was so worried you'd be disappointed you weren't going to be a grandmother."

The words wash over me like waves.

I look at Ashley. She is grinding her teeth, a nervous habit she's had since she's had teeth.

"Are you very sad?" she asks.

Very sad?

The thing I am feeling is not sadness. It is a swelling in my chest, like a balloon being inflated. This strange thing – is it happiness?

I look at Ashley and, far behind her, I see her graduation picture. For the first time, I see how much older she's gotten.

"Ashley, I am so proud of you."

She smiles, and the small lines crinkle around her eyes.

"I was hoping you would understand. You seem cut out to have been a mother, but I couldn't imagine doing all the things you did for me."

"All the things I did for you?"

I try to think of what I've done for Ashley that could merit such high praise.

I see her, just nine months old, sitting in my lap as we waited for Michael in the carpark of the hospital. I'd opened the door for us to get some breeze and she'd maybe seen something outside or heard something, but she'd tumbled out my lap and fell out the car door, scraping the side of her face on the asphalt. I remember her screaming and Michael screaming and all I could do was wipe the pebbles off her chin with my hands and cry.

Later, when Michael calmed down, he'd told me that it was a good thing I'd married a doctor, but I was in too much pain to find it funny.

I see her dressed as a present for her preschool carnival jump up. I'd glue-gunned wrapping paper onto a pair of tiny white gloves and sewed bows and ribbons onto her gymnastics leotard. I'd taken enough pictures to fill a whole roll of film of her jumping and dancing. I'd been proud of the costume until Michael flipped through the photos. He'd pointed out the other children dressed in professionally-made Superman and Wonder Woman costumes. After that, I hadn't bothered to put the pictures in her photo album.

I see Ashley's homework book returned with the teacher's red x's because, despite my attempts to help, her homework was still wrong.

"I'm glad you think that about me," I say. "Cut out to be a mother."

"Come on! You must think that about yourself!"

Ashley pulls some wine out the fridge and begins winding the corkscrew into the bottle. All tooth-grinding has stopped.

I feel as if I have to explain myself to Ashley.

"Do you remember the time you wanted to be a present for your carnival jump up?"

"I loved that!" Ashley pulls the cork out with a pop. "I was the only girl whose mum made her costume. I was so disappointed when you bought me that princess dress the next year."

"You were?"

"I know it was a long time ago but I remember dancing on the school stage. 'Hot Hot Hot' was playing." She hums a couple bars.

"I... I'm sorry about the princess dress. It's just that, well, your father thought you would like a store-bought costume like the other children."

Ashley rolls her eyes. "He would think that."

There is something in the way she says 'he'. It sounds like an insult.

"He just wanted you to be happy."

"No. *He* wanted to look good. Wanted the other parents to

think that he was willing to spend the big bucks on his daughter's costume."

"You don't know what he wanted."

"I know him." Ashley pours wine into two glasses. "You don't always have to defend him you know. Besides, it's not like he can hear us."

I wish it were as simple as agreeing.

I wish I could alight on the memory of Ashley dressed as a present. But there are so many other times when I wasn't the mother she deserved. The times I couldn't help with her homework. Or the times I felt so angry with Michael that I felt angry with her too. Or the times I heard her crying when she was a teenager, after her father berated her for forgetting a book at school or slapped the back of her hand with a ruler after she ate a second pack of cheese curls and I locked the door to my room, a little grateful that he was pouring his anger onto someone else, even if it was my daughter.

And surely, someone "cut out to be a mother" would have defended a new baby growing inside her and not let her husband drive her to one of his gynaecologist friends who carried out abortions all the time, never mind they were illegal. Surely someone who was meant to be a mother wouldn't have let that baby go, nameless. She wouldn't have lain back on the table, let them pull her feet apart with stirrups and numb her body so that she couldn't even feel the baby leaving.

I cradle my stomach as if some part of that baby is still inside me.

"All this food is getting cold!" Ashley exclaims. She pops the microwave open and places my wantons inside.

The hum of the microwave seems louder than it's ever been before. An insistent ZZZ that feels as if it is swarming around me.

"There were a lot of ways that I wasn't a good mother," I say. "I read a lot about the best ways to raise children and I tried.

But, I was never very good at helping you with school. And I was never assertive when I disagreed with Michael's methods of punishment… And… And I was pregnant once again, after you. But Michael… Michael said…"

The microwave emits three shrill beeps and I can't put into words what Michael said.

★

I'd wrapped the pregnancy test in a box. A present for Michael this time. I'd talked to the baby while I was making dinner. *Daddy is going to find out about you just now. Are you going to be a brother or a sister for Ashley?*

I remember standing with my hands cupped under my stomach, although there was no bump yet. Michael opened the present suspiciously, as if the idea of me wrapping anything when there was no obvious occasion was a sacrilege.

Just now, baby, when he sees what it is he's going to smile.

"Are you serious?" Michael asked.

I should have said then that I was. I should have said that this is my body and I'm going to have this baby, Michael Clapham, and if you don't like it then you shouldn't have helped to make it.

Instead I let him tell me that another child would be too overwhelming. He reminded me of Ashley's fall onto the asphalt. If I wasn't doing the best job with one, what would happen with two?

When I came in from the beach that night, he stuck the bow from the box on top my head. "You are my present," he'd said. "The only present I need."

★

In a small voice, I say, "Your father told me I should consider getting rid of the baby. And I told myself that I would only go with him to meet the doctor…"

Ashley freezes, with the plate of wontons steaming into her face. Now that I've started, I have to make her understand.

"I always blamed your father for making the decision, but nobody dragged me to the doctor that first time. Or the second."

I'd told myself to stop talking to the baby once I knew we were going to get rid of it. But I couldn't. *It's not so bad, baby. It won't hurt. You don't want to be born anyway. What if you end up marrying someone like Daddy? Haha.*

"The baby would have been three years younger than you."

Ashley lays the plate of wontons very carefully on the table.

"I support a woman's right to choose," she says. But her voice is hard.

"So do I," I say. But this is not about *a* woman's right to choose. This is about mine.

"And I don't believe that an embryo is a person," Ashley says.

"What if it is?" I ask.

"What if it is?" Ashley asks. "Does that one thing take away everything you did for me? Does that one thing mean that all the time you spent cooking lunch for me every day and listening to me talk about my day, even when I'm sure that shit was boring, and sitting with me while I did my homework and loving me when I was sick – does that mean all that counts for nothing?"

"I feel like it counts for less."

Motherhood and wifehood are akin to paying a debt; you owe it to your children from the moment they're born and you owe it to your husband from the moment you marry him. I'd wanted to save Ashley from that, only she doesn't need saving.

But what about me? I'll keep trying to be a supportive mother for her. But there is no way to repay a baby that you didn't give the chance to live.

Ashley walks away from me until she is standing before Michael's picture in the living room.

"And what about you?" she asks his picture. "Are you sorry?"

"I don't know if he thought – "

"I'm not asking if he's sorry for one abortion," Ashley says.
I recoil as if the word is a slap.

"I'm asking if he's sorry for being such a shit all his life. I'm
asking if he's sorry that he hurt you and hurt me and lived like
this was his castle and he was the fucking king!"

"Ashley!"

"Oh please!" she says. "The only reason I wish he weren't
dead is so I could say it to his face."

I look at Michael. This man who was a doctor but who
brought death and dreams of death.

"I was actually going to take down his picture before you
came," I admit.

"Well what are we waiting for? Let's take the bastard down.
And his mother. Mrs 'Vovó' Clapham, so beautiful men would
stop his father in the street to congratulate him." She throws
her right arm out in a perfect imitation of Michael when he told
that story. "I mean, there are no men here to stop and compli-
ment her."

Ashley storms into the store room. I feel as if she's stepping
along my spine to get there.

She whacks the ladder below Michael with a thud. I expect
her to climb up but she's holding it steady for me.

I test the ladder with one foot and step up to the third rung.
At a stretch, I can reach Michael. He looks down at me with the
hard, dark eyes that are similar to Ashley's, but without her
owl-warmth. His sharp centre part shows the bone-whiteness
of his skull.

I feel as if I should say something to him. But I can't. Maybe
this is what I deserve – if I couldn't say it to his face I shouldn't
say it at all.

I sweep him off his hook. The cold glass covering him
doesn't feel that different from the lid of his coffin.

I look down at Ashley. Both another Clapham doctor and

another surgeon's wife. But so different from either of us. She gives my ankle a squeeze and smiles.

I look out the window to the beach. The setting sun casts an orange halo above the water. I imagine the murmur of the waves as they break, cresting and frothing before rolling themselves back into the sea.

THE BOSS

"What's your name?" the guard asks. He's wearing a navy-blue shirt with a clip-on tie.

"Nathan," the boy says.

"Nathan what?"

The boy peers at the building behind the guard. It's a three-storey crowned by the company's logo: three arrows converging into a larger arrow. A light-up sign reads SFK ADVERTISING.

"Listen to me, young man, no one goes in that building unless I write their name in this book." The guard holds up a hardcover notebook with DENNIS written on the cover.

"Nathan Peters."

The guard writes NATHAN PETERS. It is the last in a long column of names. His letters are sharp and hard; he writes as if digging the words into the page. The guard writes 2:15 pm in a column that reads TIME IN.

"Who you here to see?"

"The CEO."

The guard picks up the phone. "Cathy, I have a Nathan Peters here to see Mr Sharma."

He drops the receiver. "Second floor."

The second floor is one continuous corridor and all the doors are shut. The walls are decorated with framed advertisements. There is a picture of a blood-red hand blotting out the face of a man in handcuffs. His shoulders are slumped. The bottom of the page screams TRINIDAD AND TOBAGO CRIME STOPPERS. CALL 800-TIPS.

"Mr Peters?"

The boy doesn't answer.

"Mr Peters?"

"Yes, sorry."

A woman is standing in an office doorway. Struck by the light from the window, she looks more like a shadow than a person. "Mr Sharma will be with you soon." She gestures at a row of chairs.

The boy adjusts his suit jacket and sits. The jacket was made for a much larger man – the sleeves come all the way to the boy's knuckles and the lumpy shoulder pads are visible through the thin cloth. There is nothing for him to do but look out the window. The sky's the same heavy grey it's been all day. A black car in the parking lot has a savage scratch disfiguring the driver's side.

A door swings open and the CEO emerges. "Nathan. Nice to meet you." He looks much younger than his pictures in the papers. "Kiran Sharma," he says as they shake hands. "Let's go to the conference room."

A résumé has already been laid on the table. NATHAN PETERS is printed on top in size twenty font.

The CEO sits very straight, with his shoulders folded down his back like wings. "So, why do you want to work in advertising?"

"I want to talk to people."

"And you think advertising is the career for that? Why not be a radio announcer?"

"No one wants to listen to the radio announcer. But a good ad – people will listen."

"What would you consider to be a good ad?" the CEO asks.

"The one in your hall – for Crime Stoppers."

"And how does that talk to people?"

"The man in handcuffs – the image says police can catch criminals if they get some help from us."

The CEO makes a pyramid with his hands and stares at the

boy over the top of his fingers. "My father, now he has a career where he talks to people."

Everyone knows the CEO's father is the Minister of Labour and Small Enterprise Development.

"I don't think I'd be as good at it as your father."

The CEO reaches for the résumé. "This says you spent two years at Republic Bank."

"Yes, sir."

"You can call me, Kiran."

"Yes, sir. I mean, Kiran, sir."

The CEO smiles. There's a dimple in his left cheek.

"If I were to ask your past supervisor about you, what would he say?"

"He would say that I was resourceful and solutions-oriented."

"You're speaking in buzzwords."

"Sorry, sir."

"Don't apologise. Why don't you give me an example of a problem that you solved at the bank?"

The boy looks at his hands. His nails are bitten and his fingertips are red and raw.

"I helped a customer who wasn't satisfied with the service."

"What service was he dissatisfied with?"

"Credit card."

The CEO reads the résumé. "This document says you worked in the marketing and communications department."

"Yes, sir."

"So how is it that you were handling credit card complaints?"

The boy presses his hands into the table. His cheeks are becoming pink. "We were short-staffed that day."

"The entire credit card department was out?"

The boy does not look at the CEO.

An ambulance warbles down the street.

"Do you know I used to be a journalist?" the CEO asks.

Almost everyone knows that. He'd written a popular column called 'Nothing But D Truth'.

"I know."

"I was the first reporter on the scene when the police arrested Sunny Boodram," the CEO says. "You're too young to remember the headline. *Sunny 'The Boss' Boodram – Busted.* I liked the alliteration."

"I don't remember."

"I thought it would be easy," the CEO says. "Micey Phillips had become a state witness. The whole country was sure The Boss would get the death penalty. Do you remember what happened?"

"They hanged him."

"Not that time. Police found Micey's burnt body in a car. My cameraman got some footage of the car when it was still on fire. Two weeks later, they found his head stuck on a stake in the ground. I suppose The Boss meant it to be a warning."

The boy chews the nail of his index finger.

"Three times The Boss was charged with murder and each time the witnesses were killed. He was Trinidad's biggest drug lord. The whole country knew it. But they could never get him on a drug charge."

"They hanged him eventually."

"Too late. After he flooded the country with cocaine."

The CEO takes a pen out of his pocket and draws a red line under NATHAN PETERS on the résumé.

"You know, if you're offered this job you'll have to give HR two forms of ID."

"I know."

"You have two forms of ID with the name Nathan Peters?"

"Yes, sir."

The CEO shakes his head. "You look just like him."

"Just like who?"

The CEO says, "I'm sorry, Mr Peters; this position requires more work experience."

Downstairs the guard finds the name NATHAN PETERS. He scratches 3:24 pm in a column that says, TIME OUT.

As the boy walks to the taxi stand, the clouds burst apart. Thunder is a whip cracked over his shoulder. He ducks into a corner store.

"You have umbrellas?"

"To the back."

Small umbrellas are wrapped in plastic. Forty-five dollars each.

He pays at the counter. His hands are still shaking.

The day's newspapers are stacked beside the cash register. The *Newsday* headline reads, LABOUR MINISTER SHARMA SAYS 966 RETRENCHED. There's a picture of the CEO's father on the front page.

The man at the counter sees him looking. "All them big companies laying off. People can't get a work in this place."

It takes the boy three hours to get home.

At the table, his mother is mending a shirt. The bruise on her temple is healing.

The corners of her lips rise when she sees him. "How was it?"

"Good."

"Good?" His stepfather saunters into the room. A cigarette burns between his fingers. "Where you had the interview?"

"An advertising agency."

"Which one?"

"SFK Advertising."

"That S stand for Sharma?"

"I think so."

His stepfather laughs. "You went for a interview with Ramesh Sharma son?"

"It was good."

"If you get that job, I go run around this house naked as the day I born."

The boy says nothing.

"But I warning you, you can't keep living here for free. You have until end of next month to make some money."

His stepfather exhales smoke like a dragon.

The boy retreats to the room at the back of the house where he sleeps. His single bed is covered by a thin sheet with a faded spiral pattern. A stack of books teeters on the small table beside the bed. A candle, burnt to a lumpy stub, is surrounded by the blackened skeletons of matches.

He presses his head into his hands.

When he hears a gentle knock, he wipes his cheeks before unlocking the door.

His mother hands him a cup of tea before sinking onto the bed.

"Ramesh Sharma was the Attorney General in 1999," she says. That was the year The Boss was finally hanged.

"I didn't know."

"What's his son like? Kiran Sharma?"

"He's nice."

The boy sips the tea.

"Your aunt looking for help selling her fruits in the market," she says. "I know you want a job where you wear shirt and tie, but this… this could work for now."

"I wanted this job. I wrote in my résumé that I used to work in a bank. That was a bad mistake."

His mother touches his hand. "We all make mistakes."

"I have to know something," the boy says. "Do you know what really happened to Micey Phillips?"

His mother springs to her feet. "You know I don't talk about them things. Drink your tea."

"Did you know what he was doing?"

"He who? Your father? And who tell you what your father was doing – Ramesh Sharma son?"

The boy presses his hands around the mug. "Tell Auntie I'll

help with the fruits."

★

The market vendors set up in darkness. His aunt's stall consists of a single table covered with a chequered plastic cloth.

The air is swollen with smells. Scorpion peppers singe the nostrils. Ripe pineapple runs like a current through the breeze. The vendors stack piles of tomatoes, lettuce and peppers. A man with a bag of nuts slung over his shoulder eats some of his wares. Beside them, a woman is selling flowers. The deep red of her anthuriums recalls something. A red hand blotting out a face. TRINIDAD AND TOBAGO CRIME STOPPERS.

The moon is still in the sky when the first people arrive. Buyers squeeze fruits from several stalls before purchasing.

A group of women buy tomatoes from the stall opposite.

"Do you think their tomatoes are that different from ours?" the boy asks.

His aunt looks like she is thinking but doesn't answer.

★

A couple days later, the boy buys small plastic cups.

"Teach me to make tomato choka," he tells his mother.

She shows him how to crush garlic cloves with a stone. In a bowl, she mixes the garlic with a scotch bonnet pepper.

"If you don't want it too hot, take the seeds out the pepper."

Together, they roast tomatoes before crushing them into a sauce.

"You have to chop the onions thin thin."

He massacres his onions but hers are sliced into perfect filaments.

"You'll get better," she tells him as she heats the pan to finish the choka.

★

The next day, he displays the choka-filled-cups on their stall.

"We made this choka with our own tomatoes," he tells buyers.

Everyone who passes takes a cup. In an hour, all the tomatoes are sold out.

"If you have a plan to sell the caraille, I go pay you double," his aunt says.

"I don't like caraille."

"No one like it. Is my husband tell me plant it. Blasted idiot."

★

That evening, the boy goes to the library to use a computer. "How much to print?" he asks the librarian.

"Fifty cents a page for black and white. Two dollars for colour."

On the computer, the boy searches for pictures of caraille. The thin green vegetable seems to be covered in warts.

He finds a picture of caraille cut into slices, simmering on the stove. The pustules that usually cover the vegetable are not visible. The boy creates a poster. The words, TRINIDAD AND TOBAGO WONDER VEGETABLE rise like steam from the pan. He prints the poster in colour and then prints an article excerpt in black and white.

It reads:

Caraille or Bitter Gourd is low in calories but dense with precious nutrients. It is an excellent source of:

- Vitamins B1, B2, and B3
- Magnesium
- Iron
- Dietary fibre

The next morning, he sticks both pages on the front of their stall.

The doubles man, who sells out of a cart on the corner, comes over to read them.

"All that true?" a woman with a birthmark on her cheek asks. The birthmark could be a crescent moon or a sickle.

"There's more," the boy says. "Caraille cures hangovers."

"You lie."

"If it doesn't work, bring the rest for me and you'll get your money back."

★

Two weeks later, he carves a face into a watermelon rind and fills the rind with melon slices. People can sample the melon before buying.

A photographer from the *Newsday* is a customer. She asks if she can take a picture. He holds the watermelon face beside his own smile.

His stepfather hears him telling his mother the story. "And what the headline go be? Drug pusher's son pushing watermelon?"

"Don't talk about my father."

"What you go do? The Boss would be shame to see his son selling in the market."

His stepfather cuts his gaze to the boy's mother. Her hands are clasped in front her stomach and she's looking carefully at her toes.

The boy's eyes find his battered rubber slippers. They wait in silence until his stepfather walks away.

★

The next day, the woman with the birthmark brings him a copy of *Newsday*. There's a picture of him holding the watermelon. The caption reads TASTE TRINIDAD AND TOBAGO.

"Who's that ugly fella?" he asks

She laughs. "I can laminate it for you. We have a machine where I work."

She buys two bags of caraille and a bunch of bananas.

The boy sticks the laminated page on their stall, between the advertisements for caraille.

TASTE TRINIDAD AND TOBAGO.

People start calling him Taste. His aunt rents another table to hold all the fruits they're selling.

★

Two months later, the *Newsday* photographer returns with a journalist. "Every week we feature an entrepreneur in our youth paper," the journalist tells him. "You can look for your article next week."

On Thursday, he sees the article: NATHAN PETERS: A MAN OF TASTE.

The doubles vendor reads the first line aloud. "All Nathan Peters wants to do is talk to people."

"Taste, if is talk you want to talk, you should meet my mother-in-law," says the nuts man.

"Hush and let's hear the rest," Moon Birthmark says.

"You go put this article on your stall too?" the nuts man asks.

"You'll run out of space," his aunt says.

Returning home, the boy sees his stepfather's car. It's parked too far away from the pavement.

His stepfather is smoking inside. The *Newsday* is splayed open on the table.

"So, you's a big man now, eh?" his stepfather asks. He jabs his finger at the article. "You making big money with fruits."

"Fruits can't make big money."

"I telling your mother you could help out more around here."

"I am helping."

His stepfather tears an envelope from his pocket and tosses it on the table. "Is the light bill."

Since he started working, the boy has been paying three hundred dollars a week in rent.

"If they ever cut the lights, I go cut your backside," his stepfather says.

The light bill is three hundred and sixty-one dollars.

The next day, the boy brings two bags of fruits home. The bags swallow the remaining space in their shoebox of a kitchen. He watches from the other room while his mother shreds fruits in the blender.

His new poster reads TASTE TRINIDAD AND TOBAGO... SMOOTHIES.

After selling smoothies for a month, he walks into another three-storey building. He's wearing the droopy suit jacket but the air conditioning puckers his pores.

He joins a line of unimpressed patrons. They all seem to be plugged into some device to transport them away from the building. Eyes are glued to screens. Headphones bloom from ear canals. But the boy looks everywhere.

A large advertisement covers one of the walls, showing a picture of the Caroni Swamp at sunset. Scarlet ibises, like red rain, plunge from the sky. A woman lies back in a boat and looks at the sky striated with birds. Words rise from the water: 'Life should be lived outside. Bank online and skip the line.'

When he informs the teller that he wants to open an account, she can't believe he has no previous banking history.

At home, his mother is cutting fruits for tomorrow's smoothies.

"Your stepfather went to have a drink," she tells him.

"You know where I went today?"

"You went somewhere beside the market?"

"You are now looking at a customer of Republic Bank."

She stares as if he's sprouted wings. "When I save some more, maybe we can move out," he says.

His mother whips her head to the door as if expecting his stepfather to break it down. Nothing happens.

Slowly, she wraps him in a careful hug as if squeezing too tightly will somehow take away the possibility of leaving.

★

"You have any mango and papaw smoothies left?" Moon Birthmark asks.

"You know I always save one for you," the boy says. "The doubles man and I have a special every Wednesday – two doubles and a smoothie for twenty dollars."

The woman orders two doubles.

"What's this about a Wednesday special?" It's the *Newsday* photographer.

The boy says that he doesn't want any more articles written about him. "So, you're too big for our paper now?" she teases.

"My family didn't like the attention."

"A lot of people wrote in to say they like your story," she says.

"That's what they said?"

"Well, most of them."

She blinks as if seeing something for the first time. "One man wrote in to say you look like… like someone else. But we didn't publish it."

★

"You need to print again?" the librarian asks.

"Just looking. You have a section with archives?"

"You have to go to the national library in Port of Spain for that."

★

He hasn't been to the capital since his interview with Kiran Sharma. He squeezes into the last seat in a bus jammed full of people. The air is thick with sweat.

Eventually, the small houses with galvanised roofs disappear and Port of Spain's cloud-puncturing buildings come into sight.

A guard at the library's entrance is drinking a Sprite.

"Stretch out your hands," he says.

The boy reaches towards the guard.

"Not like that." The guard sucks his teeth. "Like this. Make the shape of a 'T'."

The boy obeys. The guard runs a metal scanner over his arms and legs. It runs along his thighs and stops just below his crotch.

"All right. Go ahead."

Inside, staircases spiral upwards in repeating loops. Paths lead to shelves upon shelves of books.

A poster on the wall catches his eye. A red hand obliterates a black face. TRINIDAD AND TOBAGO CRIME STOPPERS.

The boy looks away.

A young woman sits under a sign that reads, HELP DESK.

"Excuse me?" he says.

"Yes?"

"I'm looking for old newspaper articles."

His eyes flicker to the red hand.

"Do you have any articles on Sunny Boodram?"

"School project?" she asks.

"Yes! We have to write about an influential Trinidadian."

"You must have a thoughtful teacher. Usually students who come here are doing projects on Eric Williams."

"I already did a project on him," the boy says. And this is true. It was one of the last projects he'd done at school.

She gives him directions. He winds his way around the staircases until he's on the fourth floor.

He tells another woman behind a desk that he's doing a school project on Sunny Boodram. For good measure, he informs her that he's already done a project on Eric Williams.

She leaves and returns with two fat folders. "These can't leave the library but you can photocopy them if you want."

He settles at a table in the southern corner of the room. The folders are stuffed with faded newspaper clippings. Red writing burns the top of each page. It records the date of publication, keywords from the articles and the name of the journalist.

The keywords pass in a blur. And then he sees: Sunny Boodram, 'The Boss', drugs, murder.

He reads the title. SUNNY BOODRAM, THE BOSS OF COCAINE.

"Five years after infamous crime lord, Sunny 'The Boss' Boodram and his notorious gang were hanged, fear still stalks the rural village of Piparo. Villagers refuse to say his name, as if his ghost still orchestrates the network of spies and corrupt cops that led to him becoming the cocaine kingpin of the Caribbean."

Everything in this folder seems to be written after his death. The articles bleed into one another.

"It is alleged that Boodram and Escobar were connected."

"Ask any of the villagers. Boodram may have been sent to the gallows. But, cocaine never left."

"Boodram was married to Mary-Lynn Rampersad with whom he had two sons… Boodram also had three children with his common-law wife Sara… Rumour has it that Boodram also fathered children with his cousin and his maid."

He closes the folder and opens the second one. In this folder, Sunny Boodram is alive. But many other men are dying as the drug wars rage.

And then he reads: "A grave was dug in the prison ground today. It is said that Sunny 'The Boss' Boodram was weighed. This is to spare him the agony of a half-hanging. Yet there are widows and children along the length and breadth of this country who will think that there is no agony he does not deserve."

The red writing sears the top of the page. Date: Thursday 6th March 1999. Key words: Sunny Boodram, 'The Boss', drugs. Journalist: Kiran Sharma.

He runs to the bathroom. He does not even have time to lock the stall before he vomits up the roti and tomato choka that was his breakfast. He imagines what it must be like to die by hanging. Does your neck break? Or is your windpipe slowly crushed? Do you die flopping like a fish reeled onto land?

When he tries to walk back to his desk, his legs refuse to cooperate. Eventually, he locks the bathroom door and sits on the floor because the toilets have no lids.

He does not know how long it is before he can stand.

His table is exactly as he left it.

He closes the folder then stops. There is one thing left to do. His hands shake but he flips through the articles until he finds it. There is a black-and-white picture of The Boss in a suit with a patterned tie. His eyes are obscured by shades. Although his hands are cuffed, he appears to loom over the police officer. His shoulders stretch the jacket; the shoulder pads make him appear even bigger.

Key words: Sunny Boodram, 'The Boss', drugs. Journalist: Kiran Sharma. SUNNY 'THE BOSS' BOODRAM – BUSTED.

Only this time Kiran Sharma is wrong. Because Micey Phillips' burnt body will be found. And the judge will be forced to admit – insufficient evidence.

★

A week later, four people from Port of Spain come to the market because they heard about his smoothies. One of them is wearing a wide-brimmed hat like a tourist.

The boy admits that smoothies are sold out. "How about I let you try some fruits instead?"

They shrug. One of the Port of Spainers is already walking away.

The boy slices a pineapple into thin crescents – since the tomato choka incident, his knife work has improved. The nuts man gives him some salt to sprinkle on top.

"Tell me if you have pineapple like this in Port of Spain," the boy says.

The man who was wandering away returns to his stall.

They buy all his pineapple and some of the caraille too. He promises to save four smoothies for them that Saturday.

★

On Friday night, his mother can't make any smoothies because her fingers are black and blue. The nail has fallen off her ring finger. "I squeeze my hands in the door," she says.

"You can't make them smoothies yourself?" his stepfather asks. "You's the boss of fruits, not so? I hear big men telling me they buy your smoothies. You must be making good money. How much for one?"

The boy doesn't answer. He turns the blade of his knife down and begins slicing a banana.

"I asking you a question." His stepfather's shadow falls over the cutting board.

There is something, a filament that forms itself into a black-and-white picture of a man. He is in handcuffs but he stands, feet apart, shoulder bones almost popping out of his skin. This man is not afraid.

The boy lays the knife down, with the blade pointing out. His shoulders stretch. His hands fold into fists. "I'm not answering you."

"You not answering me?" But his stepfather's eyes fall on the knife.

The boy does not speak.

The shadow retreats from the cutting board.

"I should come to your blasted stall," his stepfather shouts from the other room. "I should ask you in front of your customers, how much for one?"

The boy eviscerates an orange with one stroke. "Come and ask then."

★

Moon Birthmark buys a mango and pawpaw smoothie. "You change the recipe?" she asks.

"You don't like it?"

She compresses her lips.

"We came to see Taste!" It's the people from Port of Spain. There are five of them this time – the boy only has four smoothies left.

"I come here for a smoothie!" It's his stepfather, talking so everyone can hear. "Where's the boss?"

The boy's aunt snatches his arm. "What he doing here?"

The doubles man squints at the boy's stepfather.

It seems as if the world is converging on the boy's stall.

His stepfather pushes through the crowd and slaps his

hands on the table. "How much for a smoothie?" He sounds more like a dog barking than a man.

"Sorry, the remaining smoothies have been reserved," the boy says.

"What the ass you telling me about reserved?"

"You'll have to come back."

"This is how you treats customers?" His stepfather spreads his arms wide as if inviting the crowd to agree.

"My customers can tell you differently."

People are muttering. They agree with the boy. He raises his eyes to the older man's. "If you want to make a complaint, you know where to find me."

The boy looks at his stepfather. He sees a matchstick man, brittle and alone in the crowd.

"Nathan," one of the people from Port of Spain says. It's Kiran Sharma.

The boy's mouth falls open.

"I've read about you in the papers. My friends say you're so successful they have to book smoothies in advance. How many do you have left?"

"Only four."

"I'll buy them all."

"Thank you."

"Can't we share?" Kiran Sharma asks his friends. "I believe this man wanted a smoothie." He asks for an extra cup and pours half of a banana and watermelon smoothie inside.

The boy's stepfather accepts the cup with his head bowed. "Thank you, Mr Sharma," he says.

★

Almost a week later, the boy makes his next bank deposit. He shows his mother the figure in the deposit book.

When she touches the page, he notices that the nail bed on her ring finger has darkened to a greyish-purple.

"Is your finger OK?" he asks.

"Of course, good as new."

There are three knocks on the door. They look at each other. This is not a house that people visit.

"Wait here," the boy says, going to the door.

"Are you Nathan Peters?" a man in a white shirt asks.

"Why do you want to know?"

"I'm Curtis, the courier from SFK Advertising. I have a letter for you."

The boy waits until he leaves to open the envelope.

On the letterhead, three arrows converge into a larger arrow.

> Mr Nathan Peters
> 10 Nolan Street Extension
> Felicity Village
> Chaguanas
>
> Dear Mr Peters
>
> SKF Advertising is pleased to offer you the job of marketing assistant. Further to our discussion and considering the entrepreneurial skills you have displayed since the interview, we hope that we can have a rewarding and mutually beneficial relationship.
> Warm regards,
> Kiran Sharma
>
> CEO

★

"Morning, Dennis." The boy drops a bag with some caraille and a cantaloupe on the guard's desk.

The guard writes NATHAN PETERS in his hardcover book, 7:29 am beside TIME IN. "The wife really appreciated the last bag," he says.

"Glad to hear. Have a good day, Dennis."

"You too, Nathan."

Upstairs, Kiran Sharma is drinking green tea, like he does every morning.

"Morning, boss."

The CEO is holding a *Newsday*, open at the front inside cover. The new Crime Stoppers advertisement shows two silhouettes holding hands – they look like a woman and a boy. Red writing reads: Take ME out of CRIME. Call 800-TIPS.

"Congratulations," Kiran Sharma says. "Vince from Crime Stoppers called. They love your new ad."

"Thank you," the boy says.

There is so much he wants to say. *Thank you for my new job. Thank you for my new life.*

"Moving day this Saturday?" the CEO asks.

"Yes, sir."

It was Kiran Sharma who'd helped them to find the apartment in D'Abadie.

The boy's mother wants them to run away, like they are stealing themselves from his stepfather. But the boy refuses. On Friday, he'll talk to the man.

Although he no longer sells in the market, he keeps his old fruit-cutting knife sharp. He imagines slicing his stepfather open like a blood orange, throwing his body into his car, burning him to nothingness.

But the boy knows this is not the type of man he is becoming.

"I'll ask Curtis to frame your ad for the office," Kiran Sharma says. "We'll put it up in the corridor."

He leaves the newspaper open on the desk. The two silhouettes hold onto each other. Red writing blazes. Take ME out of CRIME.

RED

I've never seen a sunset like it before. It's been years since I thought of Tennyson writing, "nature red in tooth and claw".

I first read those lines in Central Park, at the tail end of my teens, when I was studying creative writing in New York. I'd never lived those lines until now. The sea and sky blood-soaked – none of the tourist-brochure orange of the Caribbean.

I want to stop driving and write a poem called "Red", about the real Caribbean – beating, bleeding, claws and all.

I am so busy thinking of the poem, I jump when my phone rings. Robert! I decide against answering. We'd had another fight last night and, in his gentle Robert-way, he'd said, "Have you ever thought of seeing someone?"

I saw red; saw myself folding inward until I was a pinprick of pain because I thought he said he was leaving me. But no, no, no! He meant that maybe I should see a psychiatrist.

"But I don't have problems," I said, which was a lie.

"No one thinks they have problems," Robert said.

That made me feel good. If he didn't think I was fucked up, then he probably believed I was normal. Right?

"You wouldn't have to go until you're ready," he said.

I told Robert that I didn't want to see anyone. I didn't tell him I'd seen someone before: Dr Gobin.

She'd been my Tuesday-Thursday-and-Saturday therapist for years. She would scribble little notes on her paper and ask, *How did that make you feel?*

Sometimes she made me feel better by telling me, *Trinidad*

is behind the rest of the world on mental health issues, which meant that if people didn't understand, it wasn't always my fault. She sent me links to TED talks on childhood trauma and PTSD and those made me feel better because there were lots of children who'd had fathers like mine.

But most times she made me feel as if I was a pannist on stage and I had to hit just the right notes to impress her, so I started lying – lying and lying, saying that I felt normal things and thought normal thoughts.

How could I tell Robert that the woman he's dating is already the product of therapy – that this is me *better*. No way. If I do write a red poem, I won't show it to Robert. He would prefer a girlfriend who writes about daffodils and all that romantic shit.

But that's not me.

Robert was probably calling to ask me to pick up a dozen eggs on the way home. I can't forget to do that because it will only confirm that I can't complete normal tasks.

Perhaps I should buy us some alcohol as well. Red wine. Or maybe rosé – something to tie a bow over last night and say the fight is over and we can get back to drinking straight from the bottle and cooking breakfasts that consist almost exclusively of carbs.

Maybe I can be a pink woman for Robert tonight.

★

But this sun is not setting on a world of soft pinks. I walk into the grocery. A woman is bawling at a man who seems to be the store manager.

"I'm telling you I bought the brownie here! And look! When I bit it! Glass!" The woman is pinching something between her fingers. I see a glint.

"Madam, I spoke with the supplier on the phone and they have agreed to offer you a replacement brownie and to – "

"You think I want a *replacement* brownie! My mouth was *bleeding*!"

I am one of many people transfixed by the scene.

"Madam, if you would like to step into my office – "

"You think I want to step into your *kiss-me-ass* office and hear about another *blasted* brownie? I am going to sue this *mother ass* grocery and your *mother ass* suppliers for negligence!" The woman is panting.

Her words surprise me. It's as if the mask is slipping off – as if she's ripping it off for all of us – total strangers – to see the monster that she is.

Total strangers are agreeing.

"No customer service," a man in a plaid shirt is saying.

"If you don't cuss down the place, these people don't give a damn," mutters a woman with a basket full of fruits.

"You should light them up on Facebook!"

"P-p-lease there's no-no need…" the manager stammers.

I look out the window at the slaughterhouse sunset. Why is it that when this woman goes mad, these people think it's OK? But when I do, Robert thinks there's something wrong with me?

Yesterday, he suggested we go over to my mother's for dinner and of course I panicked. I didn't want her telling Robert about my father, or the time she cleaned my shower because I thought things would be easier if I just cut my wrists. That happened after a low, low period and I regretted it immediately. I bled like crazy and called for help because it hurt.

My last boyfriend threw stuff she told him back in my face after our break-up; called me a *psycho bitch* loud enough for the neighbours to hear.

So maybe I got a bit hysterical when Robert suggested dinner at my mother's. And he didn't even try to understand me, like these people were doing with this woman who found a piece of glass in her brownie.

Has Robert become so fed up with me that he can't be empathetic?

I want to sit down because I'm breathing so hard I'm starting to hiccough.

"Excuse me," I say as I push outside the grocery. The car is a long way away, so I plop down on the ground and try the breathing trick that Dr Gobin taught me. I'm supposed to breathe in through my nose but I can't quite manage it. I breathe in through my mouth.

Dr Gobin said that I should hold the breath in my belly and not my chest. My belly doesn't want any air. I feel the breath pummelling my chest because it won't sink any lower.

I imagine Robert calling my mother right now. We probably don't need eggs; he just wanted to keep me out of the house so he can ask her about my childhood.

I realise that I am panting.

"Excuse me, are you OK?" It is the total stranger who worried that the woman who ate the glass was receiving poor customer service.

"Yes sir," I say. "I just have to tie my shoes."

I'm wearing slippers but I stick out a foot and pretend to tie a bow. I keep faking the knot until I hear his steps retreat.

I need to breathe slow through my nose, hold the breath in my belly, then breathe out through my mouth. Dr Gobin told me to make a small hole in my lips as if I were trying to drink through a straw. Instead of sucking in, I blow out.

There is the sound of slapping. I jump. A woman is approaching and her feet are slapping the ground, *whap whap whap*. Why does she look so familiar?

I remember now... she's the woman who ate the glass. Did she... I can't remember what happened because I left, because I was worried about Robert, because he doesn't always feel sorry for me, like those people were for this woman.

I feel like I've solved a puzzle. My breathing is almost back to normal and I am going to get up and walk into the grocery and buy eggs because I can do it.

I read the hanging signs over the aisles until I see the word EGGS. There are so many eggs, so many brands. I choose some that are brown and speckled. They look like the kind a normal woman brings back from the grocery.

Maybe those people felt empathy for the woman because she was hurt and it wasn't her fault?

I duck into the next aisle and walk as if I'm browsing.

Maybe if I pace up and down at night it's my fault; or if I don't want Robert to spend an evening with my mother, but if you buy a brownie in a reputable supermarket and there's a piece of glass in it, that could never be your fault. If it makes you mad you're behaving like any normal person would after they've had their mouth cut up. Maybe, if I came home and told Robert I bit a piece of glass in a brownie, he would be so sorry for me that he would put his arms around me, and we wouldn't talk about my mother or my poem-pacing because now wouldn't be the time.

But how will he believe me if my mouth isn't bleeding? And wouldn't he want to know the brand of brownie?

So, what if I buy some local brownies, crumble one up like I've been eating it and tell Robert I swallowed a piece of glass... But no, how would I be sure it was glass and not something hard in the brownie? I know Robert. He may suggest it was a nut and that I'm overreacting.

I once thought I'd broken a tooth trying to bite through a salt prune seed, but Robert inspected my mouth and told me he couldn't even see a crack.

If I show him the glass he would have to believe me.

Maybe I could buy a beer bottle, smash it, and then use a shard of glass. But that wouldn't be enough. Robert won't be that sorry for me if I just happened to find a piece of glass in a brownie. What was it the woman said earlier? Her mouth was bleeding.

Was she exaggerating?

I am standing in front of the brownies. There's a local brand called Miss Mavis. Miss Mavis sounds like a nice old lady who makes brownies in her retirement and I don't want to ruin her reputation. Are there any other local brands? Aha! Elizabeth-Marie's Baked Goods. I have no idea who Elizabeth-Marie is but she sounds like a bitch.

I seize a pack of her product. They even look dry.

A couple aisles down, I grab a beer bottle. The glass is sharp in my hand, which is insane because I haven't broken the bottle yet. It's hard to hold the bottle and the brownies and the fat carton of eggs, and I wish I'd taken a basket. There's nothing to do but balance the brownies on the eggs, pinch the bottle neck between two fingers and hope that it doesn't drop.

I try to find a short cashier line but they are all so long they're curving. None of the people in the lines look friendly. One man is snarling into his phone. I hope that he isn't talking to a woman because his voice is hard and angry and I know that when a man talks to you like that on the phone, things only get worse when he comes home. Towards the end of our relationship, Jared talked to me like that.

And I used to think, thank goodness Jared is gone and Robert is here, but now Robert might go too.

"Excuse me, are you in the line?"

"Miss?" the person asks but I can't even talk so I duck my head and walk until I am at the line on the farthest edge of the supermarket. I join the line and keep my head down.

The snarling man keeps it up, like a dog locked behind a gate.

I breathe in through my nose. My fingers throb. If that's how much the bottle hurts my fingers, then how much more will it hurt the inside of my mouth? Should I put it back?

But then what will I do? Go home with the eggs, then pace up and down preparing my red poem, or wait for Robert to mention my mother again?

When things were better I used to do nice things for Robert. I would write sonnets and fold them into little origami cranes for him to find.

Maybe I could do that instead?

Or will that just make Robert remember what the good old days used to be like?

Dr Gobin told me that I should learn what triggers my anxiety. Was it Jared? Work? Traffic?

She explained that living through stress-inducing situations in childhood made me more likely to overreact to every day stressors as an adult. The first step was to identify the stressors. *Jared said that maybe you should let your hair grow longer. How did that make you feel?*

And the truth was that I didn't care whether Jared liked my hair longer or shorter. I wanted to ask: if bad childhoods were so common, why was I only one who found it hard to get out of bed on time? Who felt like crying if the boss didn't like my presentation? Who felt anxious when her boyfriend called her phone?

I felt as if Dr Gobin was getting frustrated with me, so I had to say something. I said that sometimes Jared reminded me of my dad, which was a damned lie because I barely remember my dad. Something to do with emotional trauma inducing memory loss. Except, on the way home, I started to worry that maybe subconsciously I was dating a man like my father; so I guess you could say that Dr Gobin was the trigger. But I'd stopped visiting Dr Gobin and these things still happen.

"Excuse me?" The cashier is rolling her eyes and I realise it's me next. I rush forward and the bottle slips through my hands. I squash my eyes shut and wait for the crash but no, no, it's not over yet, I somehow catch the bottle between my knees and it's OK, it's OK, nothing is broken or breaking. I waddle up to the cashier and extract the bottle and she scans the items *beep beep beep.* I pay and a man puts everything into a bag and I am done.

When I get outside I realise that the red red sun is being swallowed up by the sea.

And the sea looks so vast and greedy that it makes me feel sure that if it can swallow a whole sun, then I can bite a shard of glass and bloody my tongue up a bit and cry (but not too much) and tell Robert that Elizabeth-Marie tried to cut out my taste buds (or is that too dramatic?) and he will say it's OK and help me clean it up and maybe tell grammar jokes that he thinks I will like because I'm a poet.

My all-time favourite is,

Knock-knock.

Who's there?

To.

To who?

To whom.

He told me that before I had to do a poetry reading and I was nervous; then he said he had a joke for me and I said, now isn't the time for jokes, but he said that this was a literary joke and he was saving it for the right time and this was the right time and I actually did laugh at that joke and then he said if he could have the courage to tell me that very bad joke I could have the courage to read my very good poems.

And now I'm thinking that Robert is such a good guy and I shouldn't lie to him about the glass and the brownies, but I'm also thinking that I can't tell him the truth – I couldn't even tell Dr Gobin the truth – and she's paid to listen to nutjobs.

I wait for the ocean to eat up the sun, which shouldn't take long because just the top of the sun is left.

But I feel as if I have to do something, so I pull the bottle out of the bag and hold it around the neck and whack it into the ground. Beer pools around my slippers. The neck of the bottle is now jagged in my hand and there are slivers of glass dyed red by the sun waiting for me to scoop them up and bite down.

What's so wrong with doing this anyway? It's not as if pain is unnatural. When people exercise they put their bodies through pain, but they do it so that they can wear a thong at the beach or jump up in a carnival band. So why isn't it normal to do one thing that may hurt now but can help your relationship because really, aren't you doing it for love?

And I reach out to pick up the glass, but then I see the scars on my wrist and I remember the last time I hurt myself. I'd thought it was a good idea then, too. I'd talked to myself until I thought that logically, I was making the right choice.

Jared and I had broken up and I thought that he was right and no one would ever love me and my mother would be better off if she could finally live her life – now that she got away from my dad – without having to worry about an adult daughter who wasn't even a fully functioning human being.

And Dr Gobin had asked what made me think that I wasn't a fully functioning human being, and I said I couldn't do things that everyone else did, and she asked what those things were and I said I couldn't be happy and just live and she said most people couldn't do that either; and I said most people fucking could and she said Trinidad is behind the rest of the world on mental health issues; if people were honest they would tell you they're fighting a hard fight. Dr Gobin told me that brave people could be honest about their problems and those who really loved them would help.

But I had too many problems. After the break up, I couldn't even brush my teeth at night. I would lie on the pillow that used to be Jared's and press my face into it and smell his cologne. And then I would wake up in the morning with my mouth like a crypt. I couldn't tell Dr Gobin that. What kind of pathetic woman can't brush her teeth?

So I told Dr Gobin that Jared told me I was a psycho bitch with daddy issues.

And Dr Gobin asked, *How did that make you feel.*

"Bad," I said, because I wasn't brave enough to be honest. But the truth is it made me feel vindicated because Jared and I may have broken up, but at least he saw me for what I was.

And Dr Gobin didn't know that I was holding all those lies inside me and she said that one day I would meet someone who wouldn't make me feel bad.

And she was right. I met Robert. Teeth-brushing resumed.

I look at the shards, like maggots blown into glass ready to crawl all over me.

★

When I get home, Robert is sitting on the step. He runs out to the car. "Where were you?"

I step out of the car. My mouth is bleeding.

"I went for eggs," I say.

"Christ! What happened?"

"I bit a piece of glass."

"*What?* What happened?"

The world is dark and cool.

I touch my lips and feel the thickness of the blood.

Robert produces a handkerchief from his pocket and holds it up to my mouth. His fingers are long and slim and he strokes the side of my cheek.

I say, "I feel as if you wish I were someone else. I don't want to read my poetry to you because it will only make you want to leave me more. And I know you suggested that I should see someone, but I saw someone before, Dr Gobin. Sometimes she helped but most times she didn't so I decided to stop. And I didn't want you to spend any more time with my mother because I was worried she would tell you that, because she told my last boyfriend that and he left me."

Robert nods like I've just told him the weather's nice today.

He says, "I never meant to make you feel like that. I wish I could have been more supportive." He applies more pressure to the handkerchief and tilts my head up.

There's no way he means that. Not when I showed him who I really am. I'm someone who will literally bite a broken bottle to prevent a conflict and then instigate the conflict anyway.

"That's all you have to say?"

He says, "I'm sorry the doctor wasn't able to help you. Maybe we can go to a doctor together."

I say, "But you don't have problems."

Robert says, "No one thinks they have problems."

And my mouth is red and bloody.

I smell the rain before I see it. Soft and spongy and glittering with the light of the night's stars.

Robert tips his face up to the sky. "We wouldn't have to go until we're ready."

The night bathes us in the smooth blues of the rain and the cobalt clouds roll in waves around the deep cream of the moon.

I breathe in through my nose and try to hold it in my belly.

I take a small step towards him. He lets the handkerchief go and wraps his arms around me. I shut my eyes and bury my head in the curve of his neck.

WHERE WE ARE MONSTERS

THE CANNIBAL OF SANTA CRUZ

Every family has a member about whom much is known but little is said. In my family, it is my great-grandmother: the cannibal of Santa Cruz. Dead, finally, at 107.

I strained the rumours out of my aunts' whispers.

Apparently, when she discovered my great-grandfather in bed with the neighbours' daughter, she seasoned him with her famous dry-spice rub of smoked paprika, chadon beni and scorpion pepper, and barbecued him in bed. When the neighbours found her, they thought she was eating a rack of lamb.

There was another version which was that her lover helped her kill him. Slit his skin from belly to chin, tore his organs out and sliced his spine into vertebrae that still held fat chunks of flesh.

That's the thing about rumours; they are threads so fine, you can't weave them into anything.

★

We are driving into Santa Cruz. Bamboo bows over the road, their leaves crackling. For me, driving into the country is always a release – like having hands massage out the knots in my neck. I let go of the sounds of the city: horns cutting through the smoky sunrise, cell phones keening for attention, machinery clanking as the next high-rise is built.

Aunt Willow is behind the wheel. I had made her promise that my presence on the trip be kept a secret from my mother.

My mother never spoke my great-grandmother's name, and if Aunt Willow ever did, my mother made the sign of the cross on her brow. She lives in a world where a frog on the doorstep means that she has to anoint the corners of our house with holy water. St Michael, silver sword in hand, stands on the devil's head outside her door. Fortunately for my plans, the rumours are enough to keep her away from the house in Santa Cruz.

"If the house is in a good enough condition, do you think I could move there?" I ask. I really couldn't bear living any longer with a woman who sees spirits where I see crows and who prods into my dreams asking, *Did you see a man? What were his eyes like?*

"You know your mother doesn't want you to move out until you're married."

"Auntie, I'm twenty-eight." I know Aunt Willow is sympathetic. She moved out from her own mother's house as soon as she could afford it. She understands the strain of saying the rosary every night. "Maybe you can talk to her."

We pass the Santa Cruz Fire Station behind its heavy metal wrought-iron fence. Then the road narrows; gravel and dirt gnawing away at its edges. Clumps of crab grass explode from the earth. The air feels wetter and heavier.

"We'll see," my aunt says eventually – as if the conversation had not ground to a halt a few miles back.

We turn down a road that is almost entirely dirt. Mango-swollen branches filter the sunlight so that it is golden-green. It takes a while to spot the wood and galvanize house that is almost engulfed by bush.

"Do you really want to live here?" my aunt asks.

In front of the house, concrete blocks mark out a small herb garden. I stoop and breathe the searing scent of the chadon beni, and the softer smells of the basil.

"I could keep this garden up," I say.

I pluck some chadon beni leaves. They slice into my finger and draw blood. Their serrated edges don't just look like teeth. I suck my finger, taste metallic sourness seasoned with spice.

Aunt Willow shakes her head. At least she is not my mother; she would have thought the cut was a sign.

Inside the house, sunlight pours through the jalousies. Plastic-covered furniture glitters. Glass figurines are everywhere.

On a window sill, a carving of a crow, with eyes painted yellow, spreads its wings. On a wooden shelf, a swan's long neck makes a u-shape so that its head bows into its breast.

"I could live here," I say to Aunt Willow. "Although I'd take the plastic off the couches."

She nods vaguely. "We need to sort through her things. No one is really sure what she has." I know that none of her family kept in touch with her. I think if she wasn't crazy before, she'd go crazy here alone while her family pretended she had ceased to exist. I am surprised by how angry this thought makes me.

Aunt Willow and I move from room to room, searching for anything like a safe or important-looking papers. I find some cardboard boxes underneath the double bed and pull them into the living room. Aunt Willow is sifting through some files.

The first box smells of crumbling cardboard and mildew. Inside, there are papers, thrown in, it seems, at random. Chicken-scratch writing scrawls across the pages, often breaking the boundaries of the lines.

I lift more papers out and discover yellowing envelopes between the sheets. I open one and see a letter written in a different hand.

My dear Annabelle,

You would not like Port of Spain. The people are too busy. They believe in nothing besides the dollar. If they go to church or the temple or the mosque, this is a hurried gesture, done more to say that they have done it than because it nourishes their spirits.

This makes my work easier, though. More on that

when I come back. I have to go but I wanted to write this note to let you know that you are always in my thoughts. I hope you are not too lonely without me.

I have been in all the shops buying glass figurines that you don't have. They are all wrapped in newspaper and waiting to be brought back to you.

With undying love,
Walter

"What was my great-grandfather's name?" I ask Aunt Willow.

She pauses with her index finger wedged between two pages. "Quentin? Quintin? Something like that?"

She returns to the papers and then raises her head like a dog hearing a whistle.

"Why you ask?"

"Because I know nothing about my great-grandmother or about… what happened."

Aunt Willow considers this carefully. "No one really knows," she says eventually. "The villagers, they have ideas of course."

"You know what they say?"

"They say he used to lock himself in their bedroom with the neighbour's teenage daughter. That your great-grandmother took a lagahoo for a lover."

"A lagahoo?" I know the legends but how is it possible that people still believe in such things? I can't find it in me to believe in anything at all. The letter suggests something rather more innocent – like a hidden love affair.

When Aunt Willow's immersed in the files again, I slip the letter from Walter into my purse.

Another box contains glass figurines. Some are broken. I see what looks like a goat's head. A clown's hat is intact but the rest of the clown is nowhere to be found.

The third box contains an old clock whose hands are stuck at a quarter to three. A mirror is wrapped in plastic and I see myself, distorted, through the plastic creases. It makes me look as if frown lines are already rumpling my forehead. I unwrap the mirror and, now, my molasses-syrup skin looks smoother and damper than usual. I smile but my reflection doesn't.

"What's that?" Aunt Willow asks.

I hold the mirror up to her but my reflection remains.

She dashes over and seizes it. "It's just a portrait of her," she mutters. "The artist was very good." She rewraps the portrait rapidly.

I want to say the obvious – that it could have been a portrait of me. I want to see it again. How could I have thought it was a mirror?

"There's nothing here," Aunt Willow says. "Just what's left behind by an old, mad woman."

"If she was mad, why didn't you all put her in St Ann's?"

"In those days, St Ann's wasn't the best place," Aunt Willow says. "My mother and your mother didn't like the idea of putting her there."

"They thought she would get worse?"

"They thought it would look bad."

I could see how a woman like my mother could come to that conclusion.

"And you thought that was a good idea too?" I ask.

"You know your Mom and I don't always see eye to eye."

I am sure, then, that Aunt Willow will help me get away.

★

I'd thought that my mother would see me off with vials of holy water and a picture of Jesus' sacred heart. Instead she says, "What will be, will be", and closes the door while my boxes are still on the step.

Aunt Willow helps me haul them to my old Rover. The car is twenty-five years old and suffers from all the afflictions of old age – no air conditioning, peeling paint, overheating, stalling and occasionally belching out white smoke.

"You sure you don't want me to drive you?" Aunt Willow asks.

"You've done so much already."

"If you ever need any help, call me," she says.

★

On my first night in my house, I dream of a man with dark red eyes – so dark they are almost black. His hair curls down the nape of his neck and his muscled shoulders stretch his shirt.

He is carving something with a knife. Meat. Red and raw. His blade opens flesh. He tears sinew from bone. Chadon beni peppers the air; there's a smell almost like cinnamon. Burning wood smoulders and smokes.

When he turns to look at me, his eyes are like painted glass with marble pupils inside.

★

It only takes a couple weeks to fall into my new routine. I wake up earlier to drive to work – the Santa Cruz traffic is hellish. I cook every other day with herbs from the garden.

Each day takes the dream further away from me, until, finally, I can sleep with the lights off again.

But when on Sunday, I drive to the Santa Cruz Green Market, no one talks to me. I hear them behind my back though.

Looks just like… have to throw rice at her door…

Throw rice at my door? What am I? A soucouyant who will have to stoop to collect each grain?

What is the problem? I have the gall to look like a woman they think, absurdly, who ate someone's husband?

I buy sliced chicken breast from two vendors who will not meet my eyes. As I turn away, their whispers begin.

Can't stop. Once you get a taste of it… I'm telling you, Mabel, like ribs of lamb…

I begin to wonder about the wisdom of my move. Did I move away from my mother to live in a community of people enslaved by similar beliefs? Still, I wish at least one of the market people would talk to me.

I do something I've never done before. The next Friday, I ask the girls who go for after-work drinks if I can join them.

I drink too much that night – no doubt because I know I'm not going home to find my mother waiting up for me.

"You're OK to drive?" Chantal asks.

"Of course." I pull my car keys out and dangle them as if this proves my road-readiness. "Let's do this again soon."

I have to concentrate on the road – sometimes the white lines seem to dance to the edge of my vision. How much had I really had to drink? One beer blurred into another.

A car tears out of the gas station and I have to stomp on the brakes. The wheels screech and I wait for the crash. I manage to stop a few feet away. My throat feels closed. I make myself breathe out slowly. My hand on the wheel is shaking. I count slowly to three then allow myself to drive again.

The buildings waver as if I am seeing them through smoke. In the distance, I see mist on the mountains. Is it foggy here too, or am I just drunk? I roll slowly around the roundabout where Long Circular Road cuts in. A black car is behind me. I realise I have seen it before. Around the Savannah? I can tell from the licence plate number that it is even older than mine. It is in much better condition, though. The fender glistens silver in the moonlight. I wonder how far the driver is going.

I am almost into Santa Cruz when I notice steam rising from the bonnet of my car. Could that be what I saw as mist? I don't want to look at the dashboard to see if the car is overheating. If I can just drive home, I'll call the mechanic tomorrow. I feel the silence and turn the radio on.

When I make myself look at the temperature gauge, the needle is well above the red line. Maybe I shouldn't risk driving into Santa Cruz? What if I stalled on that serpentine road? But what else can I do? Driving back to my mother's would be just as hard.

Should I call Aunt Willow on my cell? It's much too late, and besides, the Rover is still puttering along, though as I begin the ascent to Santa Cruz, I have visions of the engine cutting out and the car rolling down the hill.

In my rear-view mirror, I see the black car still behind me. Could the driver be following me? What rubbish. Criminals don't drive old, slow cars made before they were born.

As I turn into Santa Cruz, with the black car now close behind, I wave for it to overtake but it doesn't. Maybe it just can't accelerate.

I pass the fire station, which seems hunched over the trucks in the yard. The lone streetlight bathes the area around it in a dim circle of yellow. Beyond, there is darkness and the raspy croaking of frogs.

BANG.

The car shudders and my seatbelt clamps me into place.

A hiss of steam rises from the bonnet.

Who can come and help now? I fumble on the floor for my purse and phone. I find only air and the dirt-flecked mat on the passenger side. I scan the backseat. I look along the floor.

I couldn't have forgotten it.

I try to remember leaving the restaurant. I hear Chantal asking "You're OK to drive?"

Had the weight of my purse been on my shoulder?

The car shudders and I realise I haven't turned the engine off. I twist the key in the ignition. Slowly, I remove my seatbelt and bend over to feel around on the back seat.

My heart jumps when I realise the black car has stopped as well. I see the silhouette of a man, moonlight streaming behind him.

As he gets closer, I realise that he is wearing one of those short-sleeved suits that only old men wear. But he does not seem like an old man. His steps are too fast and sure.

"Are you all right?" he asks.

"Yes," I say. And then, "Thank you." He did not have to stop.

"What's the problem?" His voice moves like fingers over my skin.

"It's a very old car. It's overheating."

"I can look under the hood."

I pop the hood and the car fizzles as it vomits even more smoke into the night. "Do you have a torch?" I ask. "Like maybe the flashlight app on your phone?"

"Flashlight app?" his voice is amused. "No. But don't worry. I can see."

He bends over the car and I wonder whether I should get out and look too. Time stretches silently.

"Looks like you need a mechanic," he says.

Exasperation is a sigh away. It was stupid to hope that he could fix it.

As he comes back to the car window, I see the hard muscles of his biceps pressing against his short sleeves. Even his forearms are thick and veined.

"At least this happened when I was behind you," he says in that same stroking voice. "I can push the car off the road and then drop you home."

"I don't know if I should."

I think of asking him to lend me his phone. But I don't want him to know I'm here without mine.

"Of course you should." He smiles warmly.

"I don't want you to go out of your way," I say.

"Out of my way?" His smile stretches.

"I'll call my aunt," I announce. "She did say that she'd come and help me if I were in any trouble."

"But you're not in trouble," he says. "I'm here. Why don't I push your car home."

"Push it?"

"Sure. No one would dare touch my car if I leave it out on this road. And then I'll know you're home safely."

"How do you know where I live?"

"Because I've been there many times." He says this, like he says everything, gingerly. As if he is worried the words will cut me.

I hear him move to the back of the car. "You'll make it easier for me if you take it out of park," he calls. "And put the hand brakes down."

I do not know how, but I know that he can roll the car as easily as a child can roll a marble.

The gravel on the side of the road crunches under the wheels as he pushes me forward. It seems as if no time has elapsed before I see my mango tree, boughs bending under the weight of its fruits.

"Do you have your key?" he asks tenderly.

I clap a hand over my mouth as I remember. "I left my purse in the restaurant."

"Not to worry," he says. "Your door is just wood and bits of steel. But I won't break it down. When you think about it more, you'll remember that there are other ways to get into houses." He strolls up to the door and his broad back obscures my vision.

"It's all right now," he says. "You can wait a few minutes to be sure I'm gone. Although I hope you know you are the last person I would hurt."

★

I wake up with my pillow wet. The hangover crushes my head.

I try to think of the night before but it is as if there has never been a night before.

I stumble into the kitchen and guzzle water until my stomach is bloated.

There is something I have to do but I cannot remember what it is.

The light swells and crashes into my eyes. I slam the jalousies shut and sink into the couch. I still haven't gotten around to removing the plastic.

Staying awake is too much. I drift in and out of sleep. I dream

about my garden and I smell peppers being ground into paprika.
I wake up. I dream about my mother. She says we have to say,
"Praise Jesus three times for a gentle death." I wake up. The walls
wobble. I retch but don't throw up. I dream about a man of quiet
rages. I used to wear his ring. He is bored when I talk. He keeps
his voice low but he calls me names that tear through me. The
only time he is hot is for girls. Always very young with breasts
just beginning to bud. I have to get away. I wake up. My stomach
is convulsing. I roll over and look at the clock. It is a quarter to
three. Has most of the day really gone?

Slowly, like sand trickling through an hourglass, I remember that I have no purse. No working car. No phone to call a
mechanic or my aunt. No money to buy food even if I were to
walk to the mini mart. No food in the house. No house phone
because I haven't installed one yet.

I feel my aloneness, my lack of anybody.

I make myself breathe.

My brain is sloshing in my head. I'm unable to hold an idea
for long.

Think.

Think.

I'll have to ask one of the neighbours to borrow their phone.

My knees crack when I stand. I wash my face and put on my
sturdy shoes. I leave the door unlocked behind me – I won't be
able to get in again if I pull it shut.

I walk to a pale pink house. A sign, GOD BLESS OUR HOME,
hangs over the door. Through the window, I can see a woman
watching TV. Her baby plays with his toes in her lap.

I knock. She springs up, lifting the baby onto her shoulder.
Her body becomes rigid when she sees me through the window.

"Dereck!" she shouts.

A man with only a towel around his waist runs out.

She makes the sign of the cross. I see her touching her baby's
forehead before the man slams the window closed.

I want to stand on their step and scream. Idiots! What could I possibly do to you? Instead, I continue along the road. I tell myself it is only one house. But I remember the people at the Green Market, silent until my back was turned.

Some men are playing cards on their verandah. They stop speaking when I pass.

I make myself approach them. "I don't suppose you can help me," I say in my gentlest, politest voice.

"The devil can't come in your house uninvited," one says.

They leave the cards on the table and slam the door.

As I walk away, an image bubbles through my hangover. Two voices are coming from a bedroom. One is a man's and the other is very high and young.

I stop walking.

Surely, that could never have happened.

I make my feet move again.

The third house I approach is made of old stones. "Who is it?" a man asks. His voice has the papery quality of the very old.

The old man looks out from a small oval window. All I can see is the edge of his eye and the top of his cheek through a crack in his curtain.

"You get away and never come back," the paper voice says. "In Jesus's name I rebuke you!"

"But why?"

"I know who you are," he says.

"Who?" I ask,

He is silent for a time.

"Annabelle," he says. "Annabelle Du Pont."

"What's wrong with that?" I ask.

I feel as if I have been set on fire. All this hate. These people, crossing themselves and averting their eyes and acting as if I'll turn them on a spit.

"You rebuke me?" I bellow through the holes in his stone walls. "I rebuke you, *and* your neighbours playing cards, *and* that woman in the pink house. You think you are hiding but I can see you."

I stalk up the path to his house and press my palms against his door. "You think the devil can't come in uninvited? All you have is this door. It's just wood and bits of steel. I could break it to nothing if I wanted. But I don't have to. There are other ways to get into houses."

The moment I've said this I wonder where those words came from. The man's eye is gone from the curtain. But I know he heard every word.

They want to talk? I will give them something to talk about.

★

There's a knock on the door later that night. It is my rescuer from the previous night. He stands there smiling.

"I've brought the glass figurines you don't have. Just like I promised."

I feel as if my stomach is being churned.

"Don't you remember my letter?" he asks. "I know I've been in Port of Spain for a while, but I never stopped feeling for you. It's a hard thing to do but just before sleep, I would think of you exactly as you were at that moment. I would think and think until I could see you. And then all I had to do was reach out across the space and feel the dimples in your back or the soft skin behind your knees."

No one has ever felt the skin behind my knees. At twenty-eight, I've still got my hymen. I suppose that's what happens when you live all your life with a mother like mine.

"You think I'm someone else," I say.

"Come now, I know exactly who you are." His words are fingers moving in circles on my temples.

"Don't you want to see what I got for you? We could never find a snake figurine you liked, but I found one just curled up with its head on its coils like its sleeping. Isn't that better than one about to bite? I've been looking for years."

"I've never met you before," I say. I know I should feel afraid but instead I feel as if my bones are softening. Is that all it takes? A voice like shallow water over rocks?

"Annabelle, you saw me the other night. I was cooking."

There are crescent-shaped scars on his chin, as if nails have been dug into him.

"Cooking?" my voice says, although I do not want to ask the question.

"Your favourite." And he smiles a different smile – a wolf grin with too many, too sharp teeth.

Goosebumps start on my neck and bubble down my body. "My name's not Annabelle."

"No? But that's what I've always called you." For the first time, he seems worried. "What would you like to be called? I don't have to call you anything until you decide what you would like."

"I want you to leave," I say, firmly.

He hangs his head.

"I'll call my aunt," I lie.

I wonder whether he will really go. No one with a voice like his – soft as first sunlight in the morning – could want to hurt me. Then, I remember his wolf smile.

I see a hint of the wolf but it is gone and he is all smooth edges and eyes like red wine. "I'll be wishing I were in there with you, my dear. Especially since Quintin is, shall we say, gone away. I hope you know you can call me any time."

"I don't have your number," I say.

"A number? You won't need one."

He presses two fingers to his mouth and waves them at the window.

I feel the heat scorching the centre of my lips before burning them to the edges.

★

That night I dream again. Or do I remember? In a flood that is almost like pain, I remember my husband in our bedroom with the neighbour's daughter. Naked and so young. That was a door I did break down. And every splinter in my skin was worth what we did to him.

Because I wasn't alone.

He came – coursing over the mountains like water over rocks. Leaving his footprints in stone. We let the girl go. But we cut him open, navel to throat, and pulled his ribs out.

I remember my wolf-man saying, "I would think and think until I could see you."

So I think and think. I think of the part of him that is the wolf, the predator. It is harder for a wolf in Santa Cruz, where people still wet their walls with water blessed by priests. But in Port of Spain these things aren't done. That's why he told me it makes his work easier.

I think and think until I can see his outline. I think and think until his eyes burn red and then black, and the pointed tip of his nose becomes brown. The colours swell until I can see all of him. He is cooking. Something dark and spiced.

There is no number needed to make the call.

The owls talk to each other across the deepening sky.

Already, the clouds are covering the moon.

He hears me. I know he is coming.

★

Every family has a member about whom much is known but little is said. In my family it is me; standing in my kitchen in only my skin and the sunlight. Walter has had to put his pants back on – he's out in the garden pulling sprigs of chadon beni from the earth. Eventually, we hope to make our own paprika but, for now, the store-bought spice sits in a glass bottle. A handful of scorpion peppers are scattered beside Mabel.

She hadn't wanted to talk to me in the Green Market. She'd tried to do a lot of talking since. Or was it begging? Of course, by then it was much too late for me to listen.

The door opens and there is Walter, framed by sunlight and smelling of chadon beni. His red eyes burn as they traverse my curves and creases. Even now, I blush all over.

In a moment, he is behind me. "My dear, do you remember where to start?"

My hands are already on the knife. It's a lot of work to butcher a body but he's a patient teacher. I make my first incision at the navel and slide the blade all the way up to her throat. She is softer than butter.

"This looks more promising than the old man," he chuckles.

His fingers explore my body, stroking the soft skin above my elbows and massaging the spaces between my vertebrae. "That's a bit distracting," I say.

He laughs; brings his mouth gently to the bone in my shoulder. I feel just the tips of his teeth.

In the grill beside us, the flames are beginning to catch. The wood sputters and sparks as the first fingers of smoke rise.

PEMBROKE STREET

These days, I rarely visit Port of Spain. Walking down Pembroke Street, on my way to renew my passport, I feel as if the capital and I have become strangers. There are still some of the old buildings, white-painted wooden grandfathers laced with fretwork and louvred windows. But those are steadily being annihilated by concrete and chrome. Sandwiched between St Joseph's Convent and St Mary's College – those two bastions of colonial, Catholic education – I see more evidence of the war between old and new. Outside St Mary's, a statue of the virgin weeps ancient marble tears, while behind her a new wing of the school is being built – all glass, fixed windows and vast screens instead of blackboards.

I feel my age.

I am so busy lamenting the loss of the old that when I see a young man walking towards me, his resemblance to Ralph makes me jump. It isn't that they look exactly alike, though his eyebrows are wiry forests like Ralph's. No. It's the way he walks that strikes me as uncannily similar. Both have a stride like a sailor just finding his land legs. I feel as if I should say something, but what? I open my mouth but the air is hot and dry and I just gulp a couple times as he passes me.

*

Ralph and I lived together in the first flush of our twenties, when gay men really could not speak the name of their love. I never knew for sure whether our neighbours thought that we were just roommates or whether they guessed all along. My grandmother certainly seemed innocent; when we had tea with her she was always gushing about how we must make the ladies crazy. Ralph would brush the tips of his toes against mine under the table while we admitted that yes, the ladies did love us.

We lived on the edge of Pembroke Street, but in those days the street was more sure of its identity. Our house was a small wooden thing with a tiny veranda opening onto an even tinier yard, but it was tended with love. My salon was the first room you entered; its walls were decorated with newspaper clippings of famous actors, mounted in designerly diagonals on a red background. Years later, when my clientele had grown to include anyone who was anyone in Trinidad, I sometimes missed those early days and that cosy little studio nestled downtown.

The studio led straight into the dining room, which was the biggest room in the house. Ralph had brought Saladmaster cookware to the Caribbean and we would host dinner parties to sell their range. Ralph and I were a dream of a sales team. I was a born actor; no matter how many times I showed our guests the Saladmaster machine, I was able to conjure up a subtly awed voice and an eye-smile that showed that I really meant what I was saying.

Ralph loved me most at these dinner parties. We were the "it" couple before the phrase became part of popular parlance, and Ralph certainly loved keeping up appearances. And what an appearance we kept up! We had our own place and Ralph had a little red Fiat with a stylish white stripe painted on the side. I've told everyone in my life that Ralph made me a gentleman. I never cooked for these dinner parties. Ralph, naturally, let everyone know it. "Stuart didn't have to lift a finger you know; it really is so easy with Saladmaster that the dinner practically makes itself." To our guests, this may have been just a sales pitch, but it was his way of showing that he took care of me.

Whenever we made a killing at one of those dinner parties, I would tell my clients that I was unavailable the next Friday, and Ralph and I would pack our beach bags, with the KY jelly discretely rolled into his towel. Then we would drive to Maracas Beach in his little car.

I was rehearsing to perform as Othello, reading my lines in between clients, when Sidney popped in for a cut. It was a sticky dry-season day in February.

Sidney was playing the part of Iago – well-suited as he was to the role – as an insufferable rumourmonger in real life. Sidney loved hinting that he knew something that you didn't and watching you squirm as you tried to figure it out. Iago was simply a more malicious version of him. I would have preferred a more calculating villain, but I tried my best to play off Sidney's interpretation.

Sidney and I fell to theatre talk while I took a little off the sides and top. "Can you ask Ralph if he'll do the lights for us again?" Sidney inquired, as I spun him around to face the mirror.

"Oh, he's so busy with this Saladmaster thing," I said as I teased some of his curls into a soft fringe. "Maybe we can get someone else to do it."

Sidney gave me a look, much like the one Iago gives Othello when he tells him that his wife is cheating. "Oh Stuart," he said in a pitying voice.

"What?"

"Oh… nothing," he said with a low sigh.

"Look, if you know something, tell me now or I will zog your head up so badly you'll need a paper bag to go out in public." I brandished my scissors.

Sidney placed a protective hand over his hair and I pressed the cool metal against his fingers. "All right, all right," he groaned. "All I know is that Ralph is sometimes seen around with some rather… unpleasant company."

"Unpleasant? What do you mean unpleasant?"

"I didn't see him myself. I heard it from Marshall who saw him at the beach."

"At the beach!"

"Yes. Really, I don't know anything else."

I had two clients after Sidney and with them I struggled to maintain my usual small talk. I liked to think that my chair was a second home to my customers, but that day, as I snipped and curled, I could only think of Ralph at the beach with another man. He was away from home a lot, supposedly to sell cookware. But now, my mind turned to all the times he told me he was going out. Had he really had a dinner party two Fridays ago? Was he really visiting a potential client this evening? I felt as if someone were turning a screw in my stomach.

By the time night had fallen, I was besieged by all sorts of fears. Was Ralph going to leave me? Leave me for a woman? Didn't he care far too much about appearances? Hadn't he even suggested that I get a sex change? Wouldn't a woman be naturally more inclined to be a dinner party host? I thought that maybe Ralph was bored with me. Maybe he would prefer a businessman like him instead of a hairdresser/actor who could never understand what it meant to be in the red or in the black, and who ran his own haircutting business with scant regard for profit. Maybe he was sick of sitting through all my plays. Maybe he hated having to pretend that I was something special on stage when really I was a very average actor.

If nothing else, I thought, all this jealousy would make me a brilliant Othello.

"Where were you?" I demanded as the door squeaked open.

Ralph hadn't even had time to set his case down. "Working," he said.

"Sold anything?" Despite my best efforts, my voice sounded whiny and childish.

"Not yet, but I'm building a good relationship with the client and should be able to get them to commit by Friday."

"You have another appointment with them on Friday?"

"Yes," he said. Was it my imagination or could I see, even from across the room, his dark arm-hair standing straight?

"Well," I said, struggling to return my voice to its normal baritone, "I hope you impress them."

"What's wrong with you?" Ralph asked.

The directness of the question scared me. I couldn't repeat what Sidney said, especially since Ralph and I had been fighting after he had suggested the sex change. I had worn the wig he brought home, and then torn it up when he told me that I looked beautiful and began, once again, to suggest that I would be happier as a woman. Some of the older salesmen had wives and that, naturally, made them more respectable. I had raged about him not loving me for who I was. He said that I had no interest in being respectable.

Ralph walked away into the kitchen. "What do you want for dinner?" he asked and I heard the soft puff of the gas stove being lit.

"Anything," I called, not leaving the salon.

"You're saying anything, but you won't eat 'anything'!" Ralph pulled a pot out of the cupboard with noisy force and smacked it onto the table.

"Just cook whatever you're going to cook and see if I eat it then!"

Now he was in the doorway. "You little bitch! You don't know how good you have it!"

"You would love for me to be your little bitch, wouldn't you? Your little woman, so that all the other salesmen won't talk about you behind your back!"

Ralph's top lip was pulled back in a semi-snarl.

"Do you think that they call *you* a bitch?" I hissed. "Maybe they use other words..."

Ralph hurled the pan towards me and I ducked. I backed away, but he threw himself onto me and slammed me to the floor. I arched my back and kicked out, donkey-style, at his shins, but he knew the routine too well and had already rolled out of the way.

He turned me over and knelt on my back, pressing his elbows into my neck. "Did you mean what you said?" he demanded.

"Every. Blasted. Word."

My lip was cut open in our fight, but I managed to land at least a couple blows, leaving scratches all over his left cheek. When clients asked if I was OK, I lied about a fall on the stairs. Ralph had rubbed frozen aloe on his scratches, because he had heard that it would make the scars disappear, but instead he developed an allergic reaction that raised angry welts on his skin. I felt a perverse kind of pleasure every time I saw those lines marking his face, but I couldn't say so. Later, Ralph and I slipped into post-fight faux calm and neither of us was in a rush to disturb it.

Friday came and he was leaving at lunchtime, ostensibly to close out a sale, a sudden thought occurred to me. If I had some sort of episode, he would have to stay. I imagined falling to the floor, like a Shouter Baptist catching the power, hollering and trembling so that Ralph would have to lift me to bed and stay in for the night.

"Stuart?"

He was standing near the door, holding his case. If I was to pitch a fit, now was the time. I glanced at the floor; I knew from experience that the wood bred splinters.

"Stuart, are you all right?"

"I don't think so," I managed. "I've had a headache all day."

"Oh. It's best you get an early night then." Ralph placed a cool hand on my forehead. "Do you have any more clients coming?"

"A couple," I said.

"Can you handle it?"

"Of course."

"You should go straight to bed afterwards," he said, rubbing the tips of his fingers into my temples. He kissed me and shut the door gently behind him.

I had pretended to have a headache so desperately that I actually felt one coming on. I popped a couple of aspirins but there was no relief. Despite the pain, my body couldn't stop moving. As I shampooed my clients' hair, my fingers trembled. When I swept up the cut locks, my hands twitched, and when I was finally alone, I began straightening the pictures in the salon before tipping them once again to the side; I sprayed and wiped the salon mirror although I had just done it; I polished my already shining scissors.

I checked the clock every two minutes and, when there really was nothing left to clean, I grabbed my keys and, without thinking why, dropped the hairdressing scissors into my pocket. I had to leave the empty house even if I had nowhere to go.

Outside, Pembroke Street was alive with music. I could hear a steel orchestra beating out a tune a few blocks away. The tenors were loud and metallic, twanging violently over the subdued tones of the bass. The Virgin Mary wept outside St Mary's. If she knew what went on in the house of ill repute just south of the school she would have wept even harder. The house itself was unobtrusive, but the building was a whorehouse that catered to men of singular taste. The "madam" was a black, bull-necked St Lucian called Rufus who managed his charges carefully. The boys were chosen for particular attributes to ensure that the establishment catered for any preference. Rufus allegedly had a scouting network that extended through central and even to south Trinidad to find blond boys, or boys that looked convincingly blond when their hair was dyed. There were Syrians who were relatively new to Trinidad, Indians who still lived in the rural parts of the country and Afro-Trinidadians in hues ranging from buttery caramel to midnight dark. I saw a slender half-Chinese whore through a window, drawing the curtains. One of the boys was outside on the road, dressed in a plum shirt with one too many buttons undone, sucking on the end of a cigarette. I walked the street so many times I knew most of the prostitutes by sight. The one smoking was often picked up by a Mercedes Benz with heavily tinted windows.

Further south was The Strand, rising three storeys tall. It was a cinema that Ralph and I went to every time there was a new movie out. In fact, there was a little red car almost exactly like his parked across the street.

"Excuse me, sir," the boy leaning on the lamppost cooed, but I had dashed across the street before he could finish talking.

I saw the telltale white stripe of Ralph's car.

I pressed my palms against the glass and peered inside. There were two still-damp towels thrown over the back seats, Ralph's white and orange swim trunks turned inside out and, peeking out from underneath, a squeezed tube of KY jelly. The world pitched and rolled.

I thought of smashing my foot through the window and digging lines in Ralph's careful paint job with my nails, but it wasn't enough. I had to see Ralph himself. I had to know beyond any doubt that he had not somehow lent the car to a friend. I ran up to the box office and brought my palms down on the counter with a thump.

"Show's been going on for half an hour," the bored girl said.

"I need to see Ralph Stokes."

"Who?"

"He's inside." In those days, they ran important messages for movie patrons in a little white strip at the bottom of the screen. "Tell him that his mother is in St Park's Nursing Home. Dying."

"Oh," she said, leaning towards me for the first time. "What's the name?"

"Ralph Stokes."

Outside, I slid behind a lamppost. I thought of what I would say. The Mercedes Benz stopped to pick up its usual passenger. The whore ground the cigarette out beneath a shined black shoe before jumping in. Then Ralph was dashing out of the cinema, brandishing his car keys, with a familiar boy in tow. I took a moment to size up the competition. The boy was very dark and slim, with stupid brown eyes, much like a cow's. He looked impossibly young.

"You!" I bellowed, stepping out from behind the lamppost. Ralph stared.

"Come out to see if your mother is all right?" Only then did Ralph understand what had happened. I pounced on him and snatched the keys out of his hands.

"Stuart," Ralph whispered as I threw the keys in my mouth and tried to swallow them. The serrated metal sliced the spongy inside of my cheek and I felt blood dribble onto my tongue. I sucked frantically, trying to force the chunks of metal down my throat, but all I managed to do was coat them in saliva. I gagged, gulping rapidly and – as Ralph ran towards me – dashed across the road. Realising I couldn't swallow the keys, I hurled them over the wall of St Mary's College where they landed at the feet of the Virgin.

A couple of whores had poked their heads out to see what was going on, and one of them shouted something to Ralph's companion. That was when I recognised him. He was one of them.

They pointed from me to Ralph and I heard the whispering swell to shouting. I had never experienced embarrassment like this. The only thing to be done was to seize control of the moment.

"Saladmaster Cookware?" I spat across the street to where Ralph was rooted. "You told me you were going to sell Saladmaster Cookware!"

A couple across the street stopped to watch.

"Tell me!" I shouted to Ralph's whore, "How many Saladmaster machines are you going to take, kind sir?"

It was as if Ralph's nose was being dyed red. He pressed a hand to his mouth as if the gesture could shut me up. I was not about to surrender. To stop would be to live the embarrassment and the only way to escape was to plunge ahead. I was on the stage.

"Ohhhhhh!" I groaned and sank onto the pavement, burying my head in my hands. "Ohhhhhh!" I continued rolling my body into itself. I tucked my head as close to my chest as I could, smelling the faintly nauseating aroma of the sweat running down my belly.

"Stuart," Ralph called. I peered through my fingers to see he had crossed the road. "Stuart, stop this. Let's go home."

"Home?" I howled. "Why weren't you home tonight?" I was crying – a mixture of stage tears and real tears.

I heard a gate open and saw that Rufus himself had come out.

"Stuart," Ralph muttered, "What would your grandmother think?"

"Oh yes! Dear old granny!" I threw an arm out to the crowd. "Ladies and gentlemen, is Zinanash grandson sitting here on the pavement and this man bring me here to be a hoe tonight!" I shouted. "You see this man! He likes hoes!" I jabbed my finger in Ralph's direction. "Hoes!"

A group of American soldiers walked past and laughed. They had probably been here long enough that the Creole sounded as natural to them as their own twang.

Ralph hated anything other than Standard English. He hated seeing the soldiers gesturing to him and then to Rufus' place of business.

"Stuart," he murmured, desperately. He leaned forward to put a hand on my shoulder.

I pushed myself up. The hairdressing scissors shifted in my pocket and pressed against my hip. Then the scissors were in my hands.

Ralph could swing a punch with the best of them in private, but in public it was a different matter. He held his hands up and stepped back. I felt a moment of pity for him – this man who hated to lose face and whose personal drama was becoming a stage production for strangers. But I couldn't calm down because I heard his voice from a few nights ago: *You don't know how good you have it.*

My only combat training was in stage fighting, but I lunged forward with the scissors, remembering what I had done when I played Hamlet last year. I pranced forward, snapping the scissors open and closed and Ralph took a step back, hands still raised. Two cars slowed to watch the action. "Somebody going to get licks tonight!" a stranger shouted from one of them.

I swung my arm in a wide arc, the scissors blades catching the lights and sparkling. Ralph took another step back, teetered on the edge of the pavement and tripped. He shot a hand out to break his fall but his thigh still crunched into the road. His cheek hit the asphalt last. When he raised his head, the cheek scratches had been ripped open and blood was dribbling down his neck and soaking into his shirt collar.

Some of the whores were hooting but Rufus was silent. He stepped forward and slipped surprisingly tender arms beneath Ralph's armpits, lifting him up. He pulled a handkerchief from his pocket and held it to Ralph's cheek.

"Put the scissors down," he said to me in his thick St Lucian accent.

I stayed in my fighting stance: legs wide, shoulders broad, scissors extended. Rufus seized the scissors and stared at me. He'd seen through the shallow hole of my performance. Abruptly, Hamlet was gone, and I was just Stuart wheezing with the effort of the past few minutes.

"Do you want to go home with this man?" Rufus asked.

"No," I said.

"Do you have somewhere else to go?"

"No, and neither does he because I threw his keys into St Mary's."

"I have a key to the side gate," Rufus said. I would later learn that, during the day, he worked as a gardener at the school.

Rufus returned with the keys and neither Ralph nor I quite knew what to do. I felt as if the performance had ended in the second act and Ralph seemed to have been struck dumb with mortification. Rufus handed Ralph the keys.

Ralph glanced at his whore across the road.

"Tonight, no charge," Rufus muttered.

Ralph's whore had been observing the whole thing in a frozen sort of horror, and Rufus clapped his hands to summon him back across the street. Ralph and I crossed the road almost reverently; neither of us could believe that the night would end in such a mundane way with us driving home together, as if we had been on a date.

Ralph opened the passenger door for me. He turned the keys and we sat in silence for the short drive back home. When I glanced across, I saw that he was crying.

The next morning taught me my first lesson in love. I had thought that there would be another fight, that I would have to pack my things and go. Instead, we acted like nothing had happened. Ralph cut an avocado into fine slices, drizzled it with olive oil before coating each slice with salt and pepper. He laid two slices on my plate besides the steaming bake, salt fish and scrambled eggs.

"Your grandmother's coming for tea today," he said. His voice was low and sad, as if announcing a death.

"Oh yes," I said, with equal solemnity. "I had quite forgotten."

Here I was, still speaking like someone else. Did Ralph look outside the relationship because he thought I was too much of a performer? Perhaps he longed for someone authentic. And, who was more authentic than a gay prostitute? Someone who unapologetically was what he was.

"Your breakfast is getting cold," he said.

I took the invitation. I threw myself into the chair; slicing the avocado into even smaller cubes. I pushed a bit into my mouth. The salt and pepper stung the cuts the keys had made.

"Did you know that Sidney was here a few days ago?"

"Haircut?" Ralph asked.

"Yes." I pressed my tongue against the part of my inner cheek that hurt the most. Ralph got up to fill a glass with water.

"You know we're doing *Othello,* don't you?"

"You didn't mention it," he said, setting a coaster to my right and placing the glass down, gently.

I drank half the water and Ralph refilled the glass.

"Sidney's Iago."

"So, he's basically himself," Ralph said, smiling wickedly as if he were telling me a secret.

"It's awful to say, but it's true," I said. "Not one word of a lie, he's always gossiping about who's sleeping with whom."

Ralph regarded his plate and I wondered whether I was pulling us out of our comedy of manners, but he guided the conversation back to safety: "Who's doing the lighting?"

"No one yet. Sidney wanted to ask you but I told him you're always so busy with Saladmaster." Another bad word.

"Nonsense. I'll always have time to do it. By the way, you haven't said it, but I assume you're Othello."

"Isn't it appropriate?" I asked. We had lightened the mood enough to smile.

★

"Excuse me?" It's the boy, the almost-Ralph. He's turned back to me, walking over with Ralph's walk.

"Yes?" I ask. I feel as if pins are holding me together.

"I don't know Port of Spain very well," he says. "Can you tell me how to get to St Vincent Street?"

"Of course," I say, wanting desperately to help. "Continue to the next intersection and then turn left by the church. Oh, well it's not a church anymore actually; it's more of a theatre. Well, it used to be a theatre but now it's, it's…"

I see the old church as if it is still there, with its Scottish stones seemingly thrown one on top the other at random. The family that had shipped those stones to Trinidad still lives here but their name eludes me. It had been a scandal when it was converted to a theatre. I remember hearing my lines echo back to me as the audience leaned forward in the pews.

The boy looks at me intently. "Are you all right?"

"Of course. When you get to my age, sometimes it's hard… Haha." I am stalling, trying frantically to remember what became of that building.

"A restaurant!" I shout. "It's an Italian restaurant. Called Emilio's, I think."

"Emiliano's?" he asks. "I've heard of it."

"Yes! Turn left at Emiliano's. Keep going left and St Vincent will be the third street you come to."

"Thank you very much," he says. I do not even try to pretend that I am not watching him walk away.

How beautiful, I think.

It's only with age that I can look back on those times and see beauty. I was a wreck long after Ralph and I came undone. It took years of leaving before I left and, even then, I thought that leaving would eventually bring him back to me – reformed. It never happened.

I do not try to shake the memories away as the boy disappears in the crowds. I walk past the Virgin, past the old whore house that has now been converted to a tea shop run by nuns, past where the Strand used to be and past where Ralph had parked his little red car, almost sixty years ago.

NEVER HAVE I EVER

The balloons are already deflating. I'm on my sixth pinot grigio but even the buzz can't make this anything other than what it is – a shit show.

Some people are lounging by the pool, so soaked in alcohol that they seem to be melting at the edges.

I hadn't wanted to come. I had a deadline in a couple of days and was working on a short story that I hoped to sneak into a prestigious collection that usually published writers of a much higher calibre.

It was Indira who begged me. Always Indira. She'd painted a picture of us meeting a doctor or a banker.

"Imagine," she'd said, eyes widening at the movie that was playing in her head. "A sexy vice-president of one of the big banks. Let's say Scotiabank. He's rolling in it but he's just had his heart broken by a bitch who didn't know what she had. He's drinking rum and coke like water and, when he looks up from his glass, his eyes find you." She'd clasped her hands at the mere thought of our romance. "I hope I'll be the maid of honour."

Why do I let Indira talk me into these things?

There'd been no vice-president, of course. Is there ever? And even my twelve-hundred-dollar dress can't smooth over my love handles.

So, here I am, in a dress I can't afford, drinking on the periphery of a circle of people – none of whom wants to talk to the rest. We're the hangers-on. The less-interesting, less-attractive friends who were dragged along to make up numbers but ditched as soon as better becomes available.

I swirl the pinot in my glass and take a gulp.

The one half-bright spot in the excruciating monotony of this party is Indira in her thigh-grazing black dress, commanding an audience with one of her stories. Indira is the quintessential sexy brunette. Long hair, which I know she meticulously blow-dries into waves, but which looks as if she has just rolled out of bed. Eyes like melting tar. Breasts spilling out of her dress as if no fabric can contain them.

When we're alone, there is no one I love more than Indira. But when we're at an event like this, her natural vivacity is transformed into a manic push to be interesting.

"Anyone here going to the Netto wedding?" one of the people in my circle asks.

I'm going, but the effort of acknowledging his question and then dragging words out of my mouth is too much.

"Hey! How about we do something?" The speaker is Indira of course. She's standing on a chair to get our attention and holding her wine glass aloft like a flag.

A lot of the men stand up. I assess the specimens. Which one looks like he works in a big office in Scotiabank?

"What do you have in mind?"

My God.

Forget working in a bank. The speaker looks as if he owns one. He is tall with thin hips, corded shoulders and collarbones cutting sharp lines above his chest. The first button of his shirt is undone, revealing skin as golden as straw. Has a candle been lit in his chest? He is incandescent.

The square face of his watch suggests the casual magnificence of old money.

Rolex?

Cartier?

I smooth the front of my skirt as I stand. If heart-rate could burn fat, I'd have shaved an inch off my waist already. I try to breathe normally. When did I last reapply lipstick?

"We could play spin-the-bottle!" a woman in an aquamarine sheath shouts. She is looking at the handsome man through lowered lashes.

The guests titter – it's a laugh that says, *We're not still in secondary school.*

"I didn't know this was that type of crowd," the handsome man says. He looks around as if considering us. Naturally, his eyes find Indira who is still standing on the chair. She hooks her left ankle behind her right and rubs them like sticks slowly kindling a fire. "Maybe we can start with something a bit – lighter?" he asks.

Clouds have veiled the moon but his hair pulls what little light there is to him. It gleams wetly blonde.

"We could play Never Have I Ever," Indira suggests. The rules are simple: someone makes a statement beginning 'never have I ever'. When you've done it, you drink.

Only Indira could make stepping down from a chair look like descending from a throne. She doesn't even wobble in her four-inch heels. I suppose that's why she goes to TRX classes while I read in a coffee shop and powder my cheeks with donut dust.

I make my way over to the bar. Indira seizes my wrist before I can even refill my glass. "He's the one," she says.

"Do you know him?"

"No. But you can be damn sure I will by the end of the night." She runs her tongue over her teeth and then smiles at me. "Do I have any lipstick smudges?"

Of course she is immaculate.

"I think I see a whitehead," I say.

"You HAVE to pop it!" She pulls me away from the crowd. I claw my nails into her chin until a scarlet colour is visible even through her foundation.

"I got it. But it's a bit red."

"Better than a fucking whitehead. Am I right?" She laughs and flutters her hands around her face.

"This is my dream guy," she says. "He's Richie Rich who's going to marry me and take me away from my eight-to-four so that I can write full time."

I look at her chin. It's like the Japanese flag with that huge red dot in the centre.

"I'll drink to that," I say. "If you let me refill my glass."

Indira walks as if the air is viscous and she has to wade through it.

The handsome man, and every other man in the place, is staring at her.

She does not even look at me as she heads over to the pool. Women have already clustered around the handsome man but Indira picks her way through them. "You don't mind?" she asks the woman next to him, who clearly does. Indira squeezes between them so that her hips are almost touching his.

I feel like an elephant lumbering through the bushes after her performance. I deposit myself among the same gaggle of misfits I'd previously been sitting with.

"I'll go first," Indira says. She tugs the neck of her dress as if the thought of what she is going to say makes her hot. "Never have I ever given a blowjob with champagne in my mouth."

The crowd undulates. Indira licks her lips and peers at every face. "No one's drinking?"

"I didn't know people did that," a man with an Irish accent says.

Indira raises her glass in his direction. "It's the bubbles." Her throat stretches long and tawny as she drinks.

The handsome man is looking at her with parted lips. "Is there any champagne at this party?" he asks.

The crowd chuckles.

"How about doing it with rum?" I ask. Not because I've done it, but because I want Indira to lose that cat-that-ate-the-canary smile. "Some guys like the burn."

One of his eyebrows raises just a fraction. I arch my back – just a subtle something.

"I wonder…" he begins to say but he doesn't finish the thought.

The game continues. It's all about sex. People high on alcohol are using the game to brag about what they've done. Had a threesome. Tried blindfolding. Had a quickie in the Lapeyrouse Cemetery on Carnival Tuesday.

All of us women are looking at the handsome man. When does he drink? We wait on his turn. What will he say? What has he done?

The laughter evaporates as he prepares to speak.

"Never have I ever killed anyone."

There is silence. His ocean-after-a-storm eyes find Indira's; her cheeks stop working before they can lift her lips.

He shrugs. "Oh well." Raises his glass and drinks.

★

Of course, Indira is still going home with him. Who jokes about killing someone? It should have been enough to put her off.

"I bet he's going to be mind-blowing," she whispers as she fixes her hair in the bathroom. "No one who looks like that could be anything other than a sex god."

I don't say anything. The red mark I'd left on her chin has evaporated.

"And he's given me an idea for a story," Indira continues. "Imagine… a serial killer who uses the guise of Never Have I Ever to confess to his crimes."

"What if he *is* a serial killer who uses the guise of Never Have I Ever to confess to his crimes?"

Indira shrugs as if to say that's a risk she's willing to take. "What if he's a partner in one of those hotshot law firms?"

She applies her secret weapon – matte lipstick that she swears stays on through an hour of kissing. She smacks her ruby lips together. "It's scented too," she says. "Mojito madness."

★

I drive home at four in the morning and barely get my car door open before the alcohol erupts through my mouth. The sour smell of regurgitated wine and stomach acid only makes my insides seethe more violently.

I lift my hips and slide over to the passenger's side so that I don't have to step in it.

It takes me three tries before I can get my key into the lock.

My apartment is Siberia. Did sober me really think leaving the AC on was a good idea? I switch it off and collapse onto my couch.

After yet another one of these nights – nights that begin days before, when I go for a Brazilian wax (just in case I should find myself dropping panties for a vice-president of Scotiabank) and stretch into evenings spent covering my teenage acne scars with concealer, and letting Indira glue a forest of fake lashes over my real ones; after the inevitable disappointment of another party where Indira enraptures the crowd and I nurse glass after glass of wine – I promise myself that this will never happen again.

After I've taken off my heels because my sweat-saturated feet are screaming for release; after I've driven drunk back to my apartment because no one invited me to theirs; after I'd brought up my insides and thrown myself onto the nearest piece of furniture because the room is whirring around me, I promise that the next time Indira spins some rags-to-riches story about both of us meeting Richie Rich, I will tell her to go to hell because maybe, just maybe, Brazilian waxes and five hundred dollars of make up can't pull us out of wherever we're stuck.

For God's sake, we can't afford to live like this. But, here we are, almost thirty and still trying to get some man to love us.

★

What I called my foolproof hangover cure at twenty-one is more like hangover management at twenty-nine. Still, I have a lot to do and I can't let last night's romantic failure become today's literary failure. I turn off my cell phone and settle down to write. I churn out about fifteen hundred words, but I don't know how many I can keep.

This is another reason why I shouldn't have gone anywhere last night.

Eventually, I give up and decide to read one of Indira's stories. We're supposed to workshop each other's work next week.

Maybe Indira would be more tolerable if she was just an aspiring gold digger. But, she's regrettably one of the best writers I've read. Her only problem is that she writes herself into all her stories.

I begin her story called *La Diablesse*. Reading it only makes me more depressed. Despite her garrulity in person, Indira the writer has a gift for simplicity. Her words are naked. Literary devices are scant. Short, muscular verbs do the work. As usual, I find myself wondering whether I hide behind similes, metaphors and sprawling descriptions of setting because I really don't have that much to say.

Of course, the la diablesse in this story is Indira. Does she do this consciously? When she's writing about a demonic temptress with hair like liquid spun into strands, is she actually thinking of herself? The story's heroine leads away a man she's met at a party. He suggests his place but she says she knows a spot in the forest where they can make love in starlight. She leads him along a midnight road, her human foot walking on the pitch and her cow's hoof sinking into the grass.

I finish reading the story in a rage. Not because the idiot man is dead – he deserved to die – but because of the brutish unfairness of Indira having so much of everything – looks, personality, talent – when I have so little.

I take a tub of Ben & Jerry's Chunky Monkey out of the fridge and, ignoring the irony, eat the rest in front of the TV.

★

At my desk at work next day, over lunch, I read the paper. The headline screams DRAINED OF BLOOD. A woman has been fished out of the Diego Martin River. Both her hands and feet were bound and a black piece of rope was tied around her neck. The pathologist was said to be traumatised because the body was totally bloodless.

"Like it have vampires out here," someone says as she passes my desk.

I barely look up. The report says that police are asking for the public's assistance in identifying the body. The woman is five feet seven inches and of Indian descent.

I imagine Indira pale from blood loss, skin puckered with wrinkles after time spent submerged in the river.

How could I not call her after the party when she left with that guy?

I dig my phone out of my purse and dial her number.

God, I'm such a bitch – trying to leave a red mark on Indira's face and whining because she's so talented, instead of protecting her from a fucking psycho.

I'm never going to get drunk again. Never going to sit back and watch people make bad decisions because I'm too sloshed to stop them.

Six rings. Then, voicemail.

I don't leave a message. I wrack my brain to think of who Indira would have spoken to since the party.

A message flashes on my screen.

In a lunch meeting ughhhhhh. You want to grab dinner after work?

Oh, thank God.

Yes! I respond.

Yes.

There is no joy like finding out your best friend isn't dead.

Want 2 try Rizonni's? I wd kill for their wine-poached pear salad.

Only Indira would suggest one of the best Italian restaurants in town because she wants a salad. Visions of a four-cheese pizza, browned to perfection in a brick oven, are already dancing in my head.

Sure.

Now that everything is back to normal. Sure. Why not?

★

Indira is late, sweeping into Rizonni's in a burnt umber dress and chunky orange heels, as if it's her own personal fashion show.

"So sorry, Kimi," she says. "I got away as soon as I could."

Up close, I am thrilled to see the hint of bluish bags under her eyes. Instantly, berate myself for being so hateful. Not even five hours ago I thought this woman was dead and I'm already back to rejoicing in her flaws.

"I read an article about a woman they found in the Diego Martin River," I say.

"The one drained of blood? Can you imagine what her family must be going through?" Indira calls the waiter over with a simpering smile. "I can't help thinking that would be a fabulous idea for a story."

Indira orders a bottle of pinot and the waiter beams as if she's given him her number.

I want to tell her that I imagined that the body was hers and I'd imagined my life without her – colourless. There would be no one to paint pictures of our lives when we made it big, no one to promise me that my curves would make men salivate (though most of those 'curves' were donuts and fries), no one to write stories that were so good they made me hate her, but also made me want to be a better writer.

But I have no chance to speak because Indira is leaning across the table and grabbing my hand. "Kimi. He is *everything*."

"Who?"

"Who? Who? Julian – that's his name by the way – Julian Waterman-Pollonais; and get this: he's the VP of Wealth Management at Republic Bank. That's not where he gets the real money from, though. His dad – well you must know from the name – owns the biggest construction company in the Caribbean. I kid you not."

I hate her. Damn it. I want to imagine that it's luck but I know Indira worked for this. She pours her salary into moisturising facials, skin peels and makeup application courses. She tones her tummy in the gym and researches bras that lift and separate. Hell, she comes to places like this and eats a salad, with just coffee for dessert. And it pays off; she's sleeping with a vice-president and I'm just –

"…cobalt blue," she says.

"What?"

"His car!" she exclaims. "A cobalt blue Lamborghini! One of three in the country!"

"You mean it's not the only one?"

If she hears the tone in my voice she ignores it.

"He's taking me to dinner this Friday. Can you imagine? We're going to Prime! I've heard that two people can pay thousands of dollars on an average night. I mean, he wouldn't take me there if he didn't like me. Would he, Kimi? What should I wear? My pink Guess dress? Or is that too little-girl-flirty?"

When I catch a glimpse of my reflection in the mirror across the room, it looks as if I'm the one drained of blood.

★

Was there ever a time when I promised I wouldn't drink again? At this moment, it's hard to imagine.

When I was fifteen, I'd snuck a capful of rum when my parents were asleep and after its throat-incinerating burn, I promised I would never drink again.

That was the first of a string of broken promises. So here I am, home on a Friday night with nothing but wine in the fridge and ice cream in the freezer.

It's been four months since Indira started dating Julian Waterman-Pollonais. That's meant four months of Fridays spent alone while he takes her on a culinary tour of Trinidad. They eat in all the restaurants I can't afford and she snaps pictures of the meals for me. He always has some version of lamb cooked medium-rare, and while she'd started by eating itty -bitty salads with some chopped-up chicken, she's allowing herself cream-sauce pastas these days.

She can't resist taking pictures of that damn Lamborghini either. Cobalt blue. What a pretentious colour for a car.

All the stories about the bankers or doctors we could meet have evaporated.

All her short stories have dried up too. Why would she write when she could spend her free time in bed with a man who makes a six-figure salary? And that's not even counting his investments or his family land in Tobago.

To hear Indira talk about him, you would swear he spent six days creating the world and the seventh day resting. Of course, she's already planning their wedding as a veritable Who's Who of Trinidad. She's always name-dropping. "Oh, the Minister, he's selling a property to Julian's dad you know... Oh gosh, that reminds me of something Jeffery Matthieu said. You would love Jeff, Kimi. He's a typical Matthieu."

As if she even had any idea what a typical Matthieu was four months ago. As if any of these people had a shred of time for her before she went home with some guy who was born into money and is devoting his life to making more of it.

I bet Julian Waterman-Pollonais doesn't give one shit about her personality. I bet he's passing the time with a sexy brunette and he'll be on to his next girl in another couple months. And there's still no way to know that he isn't killing women and dumping their bodies in the Diego Martin River.

I reach for my phone, but all I manage to do is knock over my wineglass. At least it's empty.

I type a message for Indira. *So, since you've met your Richie Rich we'll never go to another party again? OK Miss Thing.*

★

Julian's working late on some super important business deal, so Indira has deigned to go with me to Denim and Diamonds, a charity event that costs a thousand dollars a ticket and is guaranteed to be flush with everyone who's anyone.

I wish she hadn't. It's so obvious that this is a charity outing and I'm the lost cause. Indira's only going because of that drunk text I'd sent last week and there's none of the excitement of our previous party preparations. In fact, Indira's dressed in a simple black shirt and jeans – as if she were running to the mall.

I suppose there's no need to squash her ribs into waist-shapers when Julian isn't going to be there to appreciate the effects. Or maybe all that pasta is finally adding some fat to her stomach and she's doing her best to hide it. God, I hope so.

"No fake lashes tonight?" I ask.

"Sorry, Kimi. I left the glue at home."

When we get to Buzz Bar, the place is packed. Leggy models in jeans and crop tops are handing out Baileys at the door.

Indira holds her glass to mine and we clink. "To happy endings," she says.

I'll drink to that.

We wind our way to the bar and we haven't even gotten our drinks when Indira says. "Look, it's Seamus!"

As if I have any idea who Seamus is.

"Excuse me, Kimi."

She sashays through the crowd and waves at a man in a plaid shirt. He kisses her cheek and she throws her head back and laughs at whatever he just said.

The bartender deposits two wine glasses in front of me. "Lost your friend?"

I wait for Indira to finish with Seamus.

"That's Seamus Weekes," she says, when she finally gets back. "Everyone's saying that he's going to be the next CEO of BP. You must know him, Kimi – "

"No. I don't. And I suppose I never will because that would require an introduction."

"I didn't think you'd want to meet him." Indira has the gall to look hurt. "Kimi, of course I can introduce you to someone."

She looks around the party and her eyes come to rest on a short man with a patchy beard. "What about Colin?"

The sound of glass breaking tears everyone's eyes to the breaker. A pink blush is burning her cheeks and she stands amidst the splinters as if not sure what to do.

"It's OK," a bartender says. How did he get out from behind the bar so quickly? "We'll clean it up."

He touches the small of her back and leads her away from the mess – towards us. I bet he moved like lightning because she looks like she stepped from the pages of a catalogue. She has the same I'm-not-even-trying-to-look-this-good look Indira used to have before she really stopped trying when Julian wasn't around.

"Are you all right?" the Colin guy asks. Because of course this model-tall goddess is going to steal my imaginary boyfriend just so the universe can rub it in my face.

"Oh gosh, yes," she says. She sinks her teeth into her glossy lower lip. "I'm so humiliated."

"Lily."

I've only seen him once before, but I recognise him right away – skin like sunlight over sand, each of his eyes an ocean.

"I guess I was taking too long to get your drink," Julian Waterman-Pollonais says. He is holding two glasses of red wine as he walks towards her. "Next time you want to get my attention, a wave will suffice."

Lily sweeps her chestnut hair off her shoulder. "Cheers." Julian touches the glasses together before handing one to her.

He looks up and his eyes find me. He tilts his head to one side as if he recognises me from somewhere but can't remember where.

I hold his gaze and glance to my right.

"Indira?" Julian asks and there is not even a shred of remorse in his voice. "Trinidad really is too small."

He sweeps over and pecks Indira on the cheek. "This is Lily," he says. "We figured we'd drop by for a drink after work."

And – I can't help but think it – I bet Indira wishes she'd remembered the eyelash glue now that she's faced with this Amazonian sex bomb.

"It's a pleasure," Lily says, holding her hand in Indira's direction. "I wish we could have met in less embarrassing circumstances."

Indira's probably thinking the same thing.

"How do you know Julian?" I ask.

"I work with him in the bank," Lily says. "Different department, though."

"Do you?" I ask. What else can you really say to that?

Julian, forced to remember my existence, glances at me. "Have we met before?"

"In a manner of speaking," I say. "We played Never Have I Ever together."

"You're the girl with the rum," he says. It takes me a moment to remember what he's talking about.

"Never Have I Ever?" Lily asks. "I bet Julian was drinking all game."

I realise that she hadn't been blushing. That morning-sun-pink is the colour of her skin. It's like she's always aglow.

"We can play a quick round right now," I say. "I'll go first: Never have I ever slept with Julian Waterman-Pollonais."

"Oh goodness," Lily laughs. She glances in Julian's direction and he raises an eyebrow – I'm not sure if it's at her or at me. Lily lifts her glass. Takes a small sip.

Julian smiles. "I guess neither of us can stay away from a party," he says to Indira. He bobs his head in her direction. "I'll see you soon, OK?"

Then he and Lily walk off – not touching but with the comfortable closeness of people who are used to touching.

Indira says nothing.

"Are you all right?" I ask eventually.

I have two choices: One. I can rub it in her face. Say I knew that somebody like him wasn't going to marry you. You scratched an itch, that's all and I bet you feel like a clown telling everyone all about your banker boyfriend when it obviously hasn't occurred to him that you could be anything resembling a girlfriend. Two. I can let him have it. It's Rich Boy Syndrome – he hasn't lived a life where he's had to care about other people's feelings. Or worse, maybe he *is* a psychopath. Couldn't feel any empathy if he tried.

I go for option number two. "What an asshole," I say.

Indira looks at me with her soggy eyes – as if begging me to lie about it. As if, maybe, I could tell her a story about how hard his job must be. He just came here to unwind. That girl has nothing on you. Etc.

Maybe she'll let me convince her. Just like I let her convince me that I'll meet Richie Rich and we'd get old in penthouses overlooking Port of Spain while we remember what it was like to slum it in one-bedroom apartments.

"Do you really think he –" Indira can't finish the sentence.

"Of course he is. Sleeping with her. That's what you were asking, right?"

Indira's eyes are combing the crowd, but Julian has made sure the two of them are hidden.

"Come on," I say. "Let's get out of here."

"But what if he–"

"What if he what?" I demand. "Indira. Have some pride."

I grab her around the wrist and pull her out of the party.

"One for the road?" one of the Baileys girls asks.

We ignore them and I steer Indira to our cars. "Are you going to be OK?" I ask.

"No."

★

They find a headless body in the Diego Martin River – the woman's ribs have been broken and she's been stuffed into a barrel. The head, partially wrapped in a plastic bag, washes ashore with the next week's floods. The reports don't say whether there was any blood in her veins.

"This looks like your type of story," I tell Indira.

I hold the *Newsday* up to her but her eyes just flit over the front cover.

"These tragedies," she says, "they don't seem real."

Right. Because The Tragedy of Julian Waterman-Pollonais is the only thing that could be real. They better pull King Lear off the stage and make way for this one.

"I'm sorry, Kimi," Indira says. She is crying again – I pull some tissues from the box for her.

I know that she won't write the story of the body in the river. She's stopped writing those types of stories.

Now, she writes about ephemerally beautiful women being abandoned by callous assholes who don't even have the decency to know what they've lost. Although I no longer have to hear about Julian, I read about him, in his many incarnations. Always, he's breaking the heroine's heart. Indira has decided that the real horror is not la diablesse – the real horror is having what you wanted, but not quite being able to keep it.

"Do you think Julian will recognise himself in my stories?" she asks.

I doubt that he'll ever come across whichever journals eventually publish Indira's stories and, even if she someday prints a collection, I doubt he'll buy it. I know that she's imagining a future where she's the brightest star in the literary firmament and when he reads her work, he laments losing such a talented, vivacious woman. I can't see that happening. Someone like Julian will always be sleeping with talented, vivacious women.

I look at Indira, skinnier than she's ever been and still crying over her ruined happily-ever-after.

"Do you think Julian will see himself in my stories?" she asks again. As if he is all the audience she is writing for.

"Indira," I say, "I wouldn't sweat it."

★

Not too long after the Lily debacle, I do go home with someone after a party. He lives in a dingy apartment deep in Diego Martin and he's certainly not a doctor or a banker but maybe he's trying to compensate for these inadequacies because he turns out to be a hell of a lover. I leave his apartment buzzing from that wonderful combination of sex and booze.

As I drive along the Diego Martin River, I see the silhouette of a man at the water's edge. I check the time – four in the morning.

There's a splash as he pitches something into the river.

KRISTOFF AND BONNIE

I hate words. A word can never really tell the truth of anything. A group of words can be forced into a sentence but can that ever really tell someone how you feel?

I love you – what can those words mean? Maybe billions of people say those words every day. Do any of them come even close to meaning the same thing?

Kristoff lived his love in rosebuds in a basket beside our bed, in letters he sent by post, even after we'd been married for years. In words and more words. It didn't seem to matter that English wasn't his first language or that I had never learnt German after all this time.

He called me anything that came to mind: *Chipmunk*, when I was pregnant with Johannes Michael and my cheeks were fat; then *Muffin* every day for no discernible reason.

I did not have his ability to sit at a desk for half an hour and churn out pages. I tried to love with my food: a pot of corn soup simmering on the stove so that when he got home the split peas would gently heat him from the inside, and the corn would breathe life into him. I hadn't been back to Trinidad for years and some pictures were beginning to fade, but the recipes were still boiling and bubbling inside me. Even in the early years, when I couldn't find our usual ground provisions and had to use only dasheen – called taro root here – it was still a Trini soup: spicy and thick with dense dumplings soaking in the flavours of carrot and onions and salted beef.

Nowadays, you can find anything in London, so I had my

pick of plantain, cassava, and eddoes. I ran into other Trinidadian women and swapped corn soup recipes before taking my bags home and filling our house with food smells.

The last time Kristoff left me flowers, it was a potted purple orchid that sat on our bedroom windowsill, as if it had always been there. I woke up a couple hours after he did, my bad knee – weak after an ACL reconstruction and then two replacements – protesting in the cold. I was gingerly placing my good leg down, slowly stretching the other, when I saw the orchid. Although it was winter, it was in bloom, outrageously purple against the grey London sky. I took it and pressed the petals to my face, feeling their coldness and their softness.

We had a heated greenhouse behind our flat and I would spend hours loving my plants. I would readjust the greenhouse thermostat almost manically, although the electric heater was set to come on when the temperature dropped too much. I wrapped my plant pots in old scarves so that they would be extra warm. I was taking the orchid downstairs, having just thrown a robe over my night clothes, when I saw the girl standing at the gate. The first thing that struck me was that she looked almost twig-like. I had looked like that once, when Kristoff had married me. In our wedding pictures, the dress cannot pinch my waist enough and my shoulder bones are visible through the silk sleeves.

The girl was clutching a small brown bag at her side and staring in.

"Can I help you?" I asked.

"I looking for Kristoff Baumann."

The Trinidadian accent surprised me. I stared harder at her, wondering how they had met. She had a nose that seemed fused into her face at its bridge, but suddenly kicked out at the nostrils; she had long fawn's eyelashes and wet, brown eyes.

"Mr Baumann is at the office," I said. "How can I help you?"

"But, is a Saturday."

"Excuse me?"

"Is a Saturday," she repeated. "He don't usually work on a Saturday."

"He doesn't, no," I said, feeling almost English compared to this girl. I walked towards the gate and looked at her. From a distance, she could have been my sister years ago. Up close, I could see that she had higher cheekbones and a shorter neck.

"You…?" But she didn't have words to finish the question.

"Why do you want to see Mr Baumann?"

"I want to ask for help."

"And can I help you?"

She pressed her lips together and squeezed her eyes shut, like a turtle pulling inwards. "No." She sniffled the word. One fat tear rolled onto her cheek.

"You better come in."

I opened the gate and led her past our frost-tipped front lawn and up the stairs. I pushed the door open for her. Her eyes devoured the framed photographs: the one with Kristoff and me on our second trip to Trinidad. I had my hands on my swollen stomach and we were both standing knee-deep in the Maracas Ocean. His head was buried between my shoulder and neck and my hair fluttered against his face. You could see palm trees reflected in his shades. She then stared at the picture of Johannes Michael and Hugo Alexander when they were five and two, with their brown heads against our black Labrador, Hunter. Then finally at the other picture when they were twenty-one and eighteen and Johannes was graduating from Cambridge.

"Them is your sons?"

"They are ours, yes."

I dropped into a chair and only then realised that I was still holding the orchid. I put it on the table beside me and waited for the girl to sit. She lowered herself slowly, placing only the edge of her sharp bottom on our chair.

"How do you know him?"

"I'm a cleaner."

"At Ernst and Young?"

"Yes, Miss…?"

I wanted to hold onto my name, but I answered: "Bonnie."

"Yes, Miss Bonnie."

"And you are?"

"Latisha James."

"So, you met Mr Baumann at Ernst and Young?" I asked, not knowing if I wanted to ask anything else. For God's sake, he was a partner and she was a cleaner. He was two years older than I, how much older was he than this wisp? But there was something in the way she had said his name, *I looking for Kristoff Baumann*. I could tell she wasn't used to calling him Mr Baumann; she could barely pronounce it. Most of me did not want to hear the words. I just wanted her to leave.

"I didn't know he was married."

"Oh really? A man of his age? It didn't even occur to you?"

"I thought that maybe his wife dead."

"I see." I did see. There was even something perversely flattering about the fact that Kristoff would find another Trinidadian woman – another black-haired, long-limbed island girl – probably after I had lost too much of the island and the only time I was a Trinidadian was when I was in the kitchen and the only time my hair was black was when I dyed it. Had he thought of me when he first saw this girl? Had he thought, this is a girl who looks like Bonnie used to, twenty-five years ago?

"And why did you come to see him?" I made myself ask it.

She squeezed her face in again, eyes shut tight like she had just sucked a lemon. Even her fingers were rolled into her palms, in fists. She slowly released her right fingers and placed them on her stomach. Surely not? Kristoff wouldn't be so stupid as to get this cleaner pregnant. He was always German in his meticulousness. We planned to have Hugo three years after Johannes and he was born three years, two months and two days after our first son's birthday. We'd decided that was that, and that had been that.

"Are you really?" I asked.

"Yes," she said and began to cry in earnest, long, greasy tears that slid off her face.

"Well, I can't possibly imagine that you're going to keep it."

She jerked her head but I brushed it off. One of the first things I had let go was the spirits of home, the ghosts and gods heaving and breathing in every tree trunk, in every mosque, in every tabernacle. Abortion was the best option, the only option really. I could not imagine my sons, the Cambridge graduate who was already an Arthur D. Little consultant and his artist brother who had already sold paintings for thousands of pounds (to Kristoff's friends mostly, but he had to start somewhere), having an illegitimate half-sibling, the son or daughter of an Ernst and Young cleaner. I could not endure Kristoff paying for this girl's spawn for the rest of his life and seeing the money leak out of our bank account.

"I don't believe…" the girl began, but I could not contain myself.

"And you believe in sleeping with a married man? Even if he weren't married, you think he could ever have the time of day for *you*?"

We both thought the same thing. Wasn't I his wife? How could I, a woman of colour too, denigrate her like this? I wanted to point out that I had never been some cleaner, refilling rolls of toilet paper in his company bathrooms. I wanted to tell her that we had met at Cambridge where I read English at Girton on a government scholarship after placing first in the island. I wanted to say that my grandfather had been a Scot who helped to restore the Greyfriars Church on Fredrick Street, and my grandmother had been a schoolteacher. I was somebody before Kristoff Baumann had married me.

"I never want you to go back to Ernst and Young again," I said.

"I can't just leave."

"You will. If it's money you want, we have a lot and I will give it to you, but you are never to see him again. You hear me?"

"Is a mistake, Miss Bonnie, but if I could just talk to Kristoff, he could help me."

"I will help you. How much do you want? Twenty thousand pounds?"

She stopped crying and stared at me.

"Right," I said crisply. "Twenty thousand it is." I got up to get the joint chequebook, then paused. Should I leave her alone in our sitting room? "Don't move."

I wrote the cheque and signed it before calling the bank and crisply informing them that a large amount of money would shortly be withdrawn. "Will that be all?" the attendant asked and I told him that yes, it would.

The girl did not seem to have budged from her seat.

"I know his secretary very well," I said. "I will find out if you haven't quit. And don't think I won't tell him to fire you. I intend to have a very long talk with him after you leave."

For the first time, she squirmed. Her back arched and her spine seemed to roll in sad waves.

"It's best if you forget all about it and him," I said. I handed her an envelope addressed to Latisha James.

"Miss Bonnie," Latisha said as she took it, "Your husband is a nice man. Lots of men make mistakes."

"I am aware of that," I said. "Please leave."

She hardly made a sound as I let her out. She walked down the steps silently and stood for a minute in front of our black gate. Then she was gone, slim hips disappearing around the corner.

Despite what I had told her, I knew that I couldn't talk to Kristoff. He would have his words as always, soothing or trying to soothe, and I would grope with sounds and silence. Only someone who really studied English could understand, as I did, how meaningless and futile words were. What could I say? *Kristoff, you hurt me.* That was too weak. There was always the hyperbolic: *Kristoff, you broke my heart.* The past tense wasn't good enough; the moment isn't over: *Kristoff, my heart is breaking.*

I think of packing a small suitcase. I imagine Kristoff coming home to a warm house and the orchid, sitting beautifully on the table. It does look nice, that shock of purple beside the black leather of our couch. Maybe he would think I had decided to keep it as a house plant. He wouldn't smell any food simmering, but he wouldn't worry yet. He would call my name and peek his head into our room or upstairs into our little library. He had gotten *Breath, Eyes, Memory* signed for me and in honour of that auspicious occasion I was rereading it.

When he didn't see me there, he would run out to the greenhouse. Planning, perhaps, to grab me around my waist as he usually did and put his nose in the hollow between my neck and shoulder. I wouldn't be there either, just the plants, wrapped in scarves and the occasional sock.

Silence.

He would think I had gone out and call my phone but all he would hear was my voicemail and the same tired message over and over.

Maybe he would even call the police because there would be no note explaining what had happened. Yesterday, there had been two Trinidadian women in his life and today there would be none. Not the lithe cleaner. Not the old wife.

I see myself stepping off the plane and calling my mother, who still lives in our old house in Arima and, despite her arthritis, insists on helping the cleaning lady. We had been such a radical couple, Kristoff and me – the blond-haired, green-and-grey-eyed Cambridge economist and his earth-coloured fiancée who was herself training to be a special needs teacher at a time when they were very rare. We had fallen in love punting on the Cam and discussing our countries and the vast, unmitigated cruelties of their histories. Fascism or slavery? Which was worse? Was there a difference?

He had folded letters into handmade envelopes and pushed them under my door when I was asleep.

He had asked me to marry him a week before I was due to return home and we bought him a ticket as well, ready to make the announcement to my parents in person.

My family had half expected him to reveal himself to be a Nazi during the early years of our marriage, as if after making love to me and my bearing a mixed child, he would turn on his mongrel family, leaving us for a six-foot Aryan wench and blond babies. Gradually, our family had come to love his words and his little gifts as much as I had. "You have made Trinidad feel like my home," he had told my father the last time he saw him alive.

My father had looked up from the antique wardrobe he was restoring and patted Kristoff on his shoulder and said, "You're a good man and a good son."

My mother agreed from the kitchen window.

"We were both wrong," I will tell my mother when I go back home. "He isn't a Nazi but he isn't a good man either."

Even as I imagine it, I know I can never go home. I can never live in a house with no water in the taps because, according to my mother, "Them Indians in power so none of these areas get water anymore." I cannot endure the heat and the Arima market, sticky with the cloying smell of too many fruits and too many women squeezed into too tight dresses. I can't leave my life as the wife of a partner to go back to an island that I do not know if I can call home anymore.

The fantasy changes. Kristoff, after checking every room, getting increasingly worried, contemplating calling the police, goes to the last place I would be: the attic (which I hate because of the cold and the dark). He would see me hanging there, with no note, so that he will always wonder. Or maybe I would leave just a handful of words: *You did this. You…*

He… He did this to me, after all our years.

My knee groans on the way to the greenhouse. The scent of my flowers covers me. I smash the first clay pot, sending splinters careening everywhere. I rip the tulips out by their stems and throw them on the ground, stomping them into pulp. I seize my gardening scissors and hack at my roses. White petals fall in choppy shards. I pull the buds off with my hands, feeling the thorns bite me through my robe. Ceramic pots crash to the floor and throw their soil everywhere. A drum beats in my blood long after the destruction. It thumps long after I return to the house.

"Muffin?" I hear Kristoff downstairs. "The neighbours called. Have you been in the greenhouse?"

My tongue feels dry even though the attic is damp and chill.

"Muffin?" I hear a soft clack. It takes me a moment to realise Kristoff has lifted the orchid pot and then set it down. I should have crushed the purple flower and crunched the pot to nothing beneath my shoes. I should not have left it elegantly there.

I wonder what he will think when twenty thousand pounds disappears from our bank account.

"Muffin?" His voice is nearer; he is looking in the library.

"Muffin?" I hear his shoes, soft on our carpet.

The rope is thick and coarse, biting into my skin like a hungry mouth.

"Muffin?"

All I have to do is wait.

ROBBER TALK

Moon swallow sun, pelt the whole world into midnight. Trees tear open. Spirits bleed back into earth. Hell split to the deepest pit. And I rise, storm without form. The last word Lucifer heard was my name, a sound so terrible it stop he ear so that now the Devil sit in silence because I come to master the master.

This country have no hangman but I am its Executioner.

My house build with bones of men who will never have no grave. I pluck women like goose and the only juice I drink is their blood.

Lesser executioners leave you in shallow grave, but when I done, it will have no body to bury and your ashes go float forever – soul without home, death without life.

Remember I am the one man make without fear. And if a Mocking Pretender like you dare to challenge me, the last sight you see is my eyes, dark and old, like soucouyant soul. The last voice you hear is mine – plunder and thunder. The last word you know is my name.

Then you hear nothing. See nothing. Know nothing.

Trinidad, I walk on water to you. I turn the earth in my palm. But I reach. I here. I hungry.

★

The audience exhales. I know the stage. I stand with arms spread wide, taking in the adulation. The theatre is bursting with patrons and every one of them is on their feet.

I see myself as if I were in the audience taking me in – the Midnight Robber: my wide-brimmed black hat casting shadows over my eyes; my lips stained a vicious vermillion – a slash across the painted white of my face; my cape, like shadow woven into cloth, dipping and dancing behind me.

The slow clap – demanding an encore – begins.

They wish! When I am the Robber, I bow to no one. So, I walk backwards, letting the shade of the stage swallow me.

"Encore!" the Dame Lorraines tease from the wings.

I sweep my hat off in their direction. But already, my chest is deflating and the swagger-steps of the Midnight Robber are shortening.

Backstage, the spell is gone and I am plunged into the frenzy of the theatre. Makedo, luminously obsidian in his Jab Jab paint, is frantically replatting his hemp whip.

Keston Victor, late as always, is shedding the last of his street clothes. His character is supposed to be caked in mud, then painted blue but there's no time for the mud. He dumps a handful of paint over his head and even his eyes bleed blue.

The other Blue Devils suck their teeth and complain for him to hear. "Blasted Victor. Who the ass he think he is?"

"Boy, I could drag Victor outside and hit he two tap in he head."

Gabriella Galloway, Catholic and three months pregnant with what we assume to be Makedo's baby, is beginning to show through her bat costume. She turns sideways and sucks in her stomach, but the mirror still shows her swollen reflection.

In the cacophony of movement, Ana sits still. Her character – the Pierrot Grenade – opened the show, but she hasn't shed her costume. The strips of rainbow cloth consume her tiny frame. Her crimson shoes, unlaced, are still on her feet as if she is ready to retake the stage.

"All right, Pierrot?" I ask.

"All right, Mr Robber," she replies.

I thread my way through the Fancy Sailors and let myself into a changing room.

With a wet cloth, I start to wipe the white off my face. I'd like to ask Ana out, but I'm nervous about how it will turn out.

Eighty per cent of the time, I am me – which is to say, a good person. But sometimes, I am Him. Most times, I can hold that part of myself I hate at arm's length; watch him perform. If I don't like it, I can draw the curtain and turn away.

Maybe Ana and I will have a good time. We can walk around the Savannah and drink corn soup under the streetlights. Or maybe she won't like me and our theatre jokes will be strained. Or worse – what if she doesn't come back to the theatre to act?

Best not to risk it.

I fold my cape into a square and unbutton my satin shirt. A black-and-blue pattern on my stomach looks like its own galaxy. To me, these bruises have always been curiously beautiful constellations of body and blood. But Makedo, who is studying medicine, tells me that they could be a sign of liver disease.

He's dropped out of university three times, so he's not the most qualified person to dispense medical advice. Still, I change alone now so he won't tell me all the ways my body is betraying me.

At the end of the show, we all leave giant cardboard cutouts of our stage selves looming behind us. I dress in the black shirt and jeans that we all wear.

As I open the door, I see Ana; the rainbow colours of her costume look even more brilliant against the white walls.

"Mr Robber! When are you going to show me your house built with men's bones?" she asks. Her teeth shine white when she smiles.

"That's not really a place for a lady like you," I say.

She pulls her Pierrot hood off so that her curls spring out. "You'd think the one man who make without fear could ask a woman out."

The other me – He – slithers and stirs in the base of my belly. I think of what I could do to her. Maybe she sees it because she looks at her clown shoes.

"All right, Pierrot?" I ask. But my voice is different, pitched between the Robber and the Real Me. I see the shiver start at her shoulders and echo down her spine.

I smell the last tang of passion fruit between her teeth. I breathe the wet sweat and green-tea aroma of her skin.

I've always been able to tell what people had for lunch. Always been able to separate the perfume from the real scent of them. I inhale her.

Ana looks up at me. My eyes are always darker than people expect and I use them. I look straight into her.

Ana twists and her gaze turns, again, down and away.

I'm enjoying this too much.

"What are you doing after the show?" I ask. "We could go for a walk around the Savannah."

"Today?"

"Sure. Although, I did warn you that the only juice I drink is women's blood."

Her head is shaking – no. Robber talk may be good for the stage but it's bad for flirting.

"Let me tell you later," she says.

I shrug as if to say, *Baby, it's nothing to me.*

She almost stumbles as she walks away. I can tell she wasn't expecting that.

Parts of me that have been asleep are stretching and scratching. I imagine Ana under me, writhing.

Maybe I can make it work.

I am still saying this at the curtain call. The audience is standing for our usual ovation, but, for once, I am too distracted to bask.

I have been here before, legs akimbo under the picture of me as the Robber – whistle clenched between my teeth, bone-white belt of skulls looped around my waist. Above us, letters arch to the ceiling, MAMA, THIS IS MAS! We've already had rave reviews in all the papers. *A Carnival cabaret par excellence…*

A radical reinterpretation of Ole Mas characters… Mama, this IS Mas and if you miss this show, you'll be sorry!

I want the cheering to be over so that the audience can filter out and leave me with Ana.

"We going for a beer," Makedo tells me backstage.

"Sorry, man," I say. "Can't make tonight."

He shrugs and makes his way out of the theatre. Keston Victor, forgiven after another sold-out performance, is already passing a bottle of rum to the other Blue Devils.

Ana, a head shorter than everyone else, is zipping her bag shut.

"No date tonight?" I ask.

She can't look at me – she obviously regrets her overture.

"Can I at least walk you to your car?"

"Sure, Mr Robber," she says. I hold a hand out and she gives me her bag. A truce of sorts.

Because our performances are sold out, the actors with cars park on side streets. Ana and I amble along Keate Street in silence. "Pssst, red girl!" a gruff voice bellows at her.

Ana hunches her shoulders and ducks her chin as if trying to make herself even smaller.

"Ignore him," I say, touching her elbow and guiding her to the wall so that I will walk between her and the heckler.

"I want a dip in that sauce!" the voice barks. The speaker is broad and brown, pinching a cigarette between his fingers and standing with his friends outside Club Zen.

The man presses his tongue to the roof of his mouth and makes a slurping sound.

"God," Ana says in a mortified voice.

One of the group is using his hands to shape Ana's breasts in the air.

"Ay, reds!" the brown man shouts. "What happen? You too good for us or what? Reds! You sure your man could handle you?"

I look at Ana, who seems to have lost a couple inches since we left the theatre.

"I hate this kind of thing," she says in a very small voice.

"Let me try it, baby," the gruff voice brays. His friends whoop and chuckle. He raises his beer bottle and drinks deeply.

I swing Ana's bag off my shoulder. "Why don't you wait here?"

At times like these, I am glad to be more than an actor. I let the darkest parts of me loose. It is as if my shoulder bones are breaking and lengthening. He unfurls like smoke inside me. The tips of my fingers tingle and the soles of my feet feel the earth as if there are no shoes and asphalt between us.

"Look, look! She man coming!" One of the men elbows another and they snigger.

I raise my chin so they can see my eyes – darker and older than anything they know.

The laughter jerks abruptly and then there is silence.

I take my time approaching. The streetlight above flickers and is extinguished.

"Is there something you want to say to my friend?" I ask. My words are wind through the trees at midnight.

My nose cuts through the cloying cigarette smell and I breathe the salt fish and bake being marinated in beer in their stomachs. I smell the dirt under the brown man's nails, maybe he's a gardener or a handyman. I smell spots of urine on a dark man's boxers.

I see the hair on their arms rise.

I lean in to the brown man and put my hand around the neck of his bottle. His arm is tense; he doesn't want his friends to see him humiliated. I yank the bottle and let him feel the strength uncoiling in me.

He loosens his grip. "Like you want my drink? You could just ask," he says, smiling with the edges of his lips as if the whole thing is a joke.

The bottle is cold in my hand. I tip it upside down and let the beer splash over his shoes. "I'm not asking you for anything."

I inhale the animal sourness of his fear.

"All right. We was just joking," he says. He holds his palms up to face me.

"What's your name?" I demand.

"I don't see why you have to know all that." His tongue is fattening in his mouth, breaking the words into unnatural lumps.

"I could find out you know – you smell like dirt and shit. That smells like Santa Cruz soil to me. You live there or just work there?"

His friends are stepping away. Their cigarettes' smoke spirals into the night but none of them is smoking anymore.

I lean in as if I am telling secrets. "I have friends there. I could find out. You might not like it if I go asking, though."

"His name is Erwin!" one of his friends shouts. The brown man's eyes dart to his friend and then flit to all of their faces. One by one they look away.

I am looking straight at him. I know my eyes are blacker than the sky is now. After exhausting all other possibilities, he has no choice but to look back at me.

I let him see all of me.

Me.

Him.

He flinches.

"Erwin what?" I ask.

"Erwin Mitchell," he says and his voice is hoarse.

"All right, Erwin Mitchell," I say.

I spin the bottle on my fingers so that the moonlight makes it glimmer green. I let it whirl away and it drops at their feet, splintering musically as the shards scatter.

They are silent as I walk back to Ana. I keep my eyes down while I try to smother the thing lashing inside me. That dark part wants to run back and break a bottle over Erwin Mitchell's head and let the worst of myself come thrashing out.

I force it down; breathe in. One. Two. Three.

Breathe out. One. Two. Three.

I let my shoulders drop away from my ears, raise my eyes to meet Ana's.

I hoist her bag off the ground. "They said sorry."

Her lips are parted and she is breathing fast and short. "What did you tell them?"

"I told them to stop."

She puts two fingers on my wrist. My skin sizzles under her touch.

"Thank you," she says.

"You see? Midnight Robbers have more than talk." I smile. To show her I'm a Good Person.

"I guess they do." Her fingers are still lying across my wrist. "Do you still want to walk around the Savannah?"

"Sure," I say. "Let's just dump this bag in your car."

When she opens the trunk of her old Bluebird, paint flakes off the bumper. "I'm saving up to buy a better one next year."

Around the Queen's Park Savannah, Ana walks on the paved path and I walk on the grass so I can be closer to the poui trees. Their trunks arch and split into a maze of ever-tinier branches – like thousands of fingers holding up the sky. The lack of light blanches their pink flowers white.

On our left, the sprawling edifices of the Magnificent Seven thrust their spires into the night. I smell the old mould festering and flowing through the stones of Stollmeyer's Castle.

"I'd normally be afraid to walk here after dark," Ana says. "Port of Spain can be crazy."

"You know, I'm not from around here," I say.

"No? Then where?" Ana asks this as if Port of Spain is all the world, which I suppose it is for many Trinidadians. But I was a boy in Matura, a village all the way on the east coast, growing up before the stabbings and gunshots made the night scary. I still wasn't allowed to wander out late, although that was for other reasons.

"I'm from Matura," I say. "My dad was a beekeeper. My mom helped with the hives and we all bottled the honey. That's why I love the Savannah – it's like an ocean of green in this city of steel."

"So, you come here a lot?"

"All the time. I go to the Botanic Gardens too. I sit under my favourite trees and read."

"You have favourite trees?"

"Of course. They're just like people. The samaan's a cool guy but the immortelle's a bitch."

Ana laughs. "Did you learn about those trees in Matura?"

"Mostly. My mother let me climb them. All except the silk cotton, of course."

"Why not?"

"You town girls. You don't know when to be afraid. Silk cotton trees shelter spirits. That's why you can never cut them down."

Ana giggles again. "You don't believe that."

"I wouldn't risk it."

I point to the Gardens, gloomy and grey under the sliver of moon. "There's one in there," I say.

"In the Gardens? There isn't!"

"Sure. You just have to know where to look." I cross the street so that I'm in front the Gardens' gates. "I can show you."

"Don't be silly. The Gardens are locked!"

I hoist myself up the gate – I do it slow; I don't want her to see just how easy climbing over is for me.

"Come down from there!" she shouts.

"Who's going to make me?" I swing my legs over the other side and drop.

Ana looks both ways, then darts across the road. "What if someone sees you?" she asks. She is gripping the iron bars; the bones in her wrist are stark and hard.

"Ana," I say in my Good Person voice, "we don't have to if you don't want to."

I lean against the gate as if it is holding me up. I let my head drop as if I feel sorry. "I'll come back over." My biceps tense as if I'm really going to do it.

"OK," she whispers, as if every blade of grass is an eavesdropper. "How am I going to get over there?"

"I'll help you," I say. "First, hold on tightly." I stroke her bird-bone wrists through the bars. "Now put one of your feet here."

I can hear her heart.

"Now pull yourself up." I see the muscles in her arms twitch as she hauls herself off the ground.

"What if I fall?"

"Baby, I'm here."

Her hands leave sweat-streaks on the metal. "Shhh," I say although no one is speaking. "One leg at a time."

Her right leg lifts inch by inch. I catch her foot and guide it to a groove. "Left leg," I call.

Her tiny feet are trembling but she listens. Her left foot kisses my hand and I lower it to a safe spot.

"Now climb down. I'm right here."

She lowers herself gingerly. "You see?" I say. "Not so bad."

We begin walking the path everyone knows. Ixora bushes, carefully chiselled into unnatural spheres, crouch as if afraid of shears shaving off more of their bodies. Palm trees rise spindly against the skyline before exploding in a frenzy of leaves.

Ana walks closer to me and allows her arm to brush against mine. I smell the wetness of the stream flowing beneath us and the brackish stink of rats that have swum up through the sewers to gorge themselves on chicken bones and bits of bread left behind by picnickers.

"This is the part that the gardeners dress up," I say as we walk through a tunnel of leaves. The moonlight falls in spikes along Ana's skin.

"You don't like it?" she asks.

"I think nature should be wild. And dirty."

"Was it wild and dirty in Matura?"

"It was filthy. Mango trees fought with each other for light. Roots cracked concrete and you had to chop them up so that the forest knew that this was your place."

"Jeez. You would think the country was idyllic. You make it sound like a war."

"It was idyllic sometimes," I say. Ana rests her head against my shoulder but we don't slow down. I steer her lightly along the path I want to walk.

The conversation is making childhood memories rear and kick in me. Matura. It *was* idyllic most of the times. I remember holding the honey frames up to the light and seeing the many-yellows shimmer in the sun. I'd look as my father spun the combs in his massive centrifuge, until each frame wept honey. When I was older, working the centrifuge made my arms hard.

In fact, Matura was idyllic until the night my father left. He told me a fable before bed, as always; this time it was about Papa Bois, the forest guardian. After I closed my eyes, he threw some of his things into a crocus bag, stuffed his wallet with honey money and forgot to lock the door behind him.

I never saw the woman he left us for.

My mother didn't cry, though. Instead, she sifted through the trash for his nail clippings. She pulled the greying strands of his hair off the brush. She squeezed his shirts until the last lingering droplets of sweat were extracted into a jar we used for honey.

"There are ways to bring a man back," she'd told me. "Even if he don't want to come."

And my father returned, with eyes that he only raised from the floor when my mother was out of the room. He threw his blanket on the floor of my bedroom and slept under the window that faced south.

Sometimes he woke me up with his shallow breathing, but it was worse when I lay in bed and knew that he was staring sleepless at our ceiling.

"What are you thinking about?" Ana asks.

"Just Matura."

"Do you miss it?"

"No. Never."

I bring the tips of my fingers to Ana's hair and stroke the strands before clutching her curls. Clouds are swarming across the sky but she's not bothered by the darkness. She looks at me and tilts her chin up as if we could kiss. Touching one finger to her lower lip, I feel the wetness of her mouth.

Her lids lower.

She doesn't ask where we are going but, in case she does, I say, "I know a place."

The parts of the Gardens that have been forced to conform to spheres never seen in nature are dropping away. We pass the Colonial Cemetery, where Trinidad's former governors turn to dust. I know there is a path that you have to look for to find. But, if you know how to ask, nature opens up to you.

"All right, Pierrot?" I ask.

"All right, Mr Robber." She stumbles and I slide an arm around her waist.

Here the grass rises up around our ankles and parasitic bird vines proliferate, wrapping themselves around trees so that they're fused to the bark.

"Tell me a story about Matura," Ana murmurs.

"There aren't any stories to tell."

"You always tell stories on stage." She turns so that her mouth is open on my arm.

I touch my lips to her head. "That's just robber talk."

She laughs. "I thought Midnight Robbers had more than talk."

"We do."

I snatch her around her waist and bring my mouth to hers. She softens, like heated honey, and spreads herself against me.

I devour the passion fruit taste of her. Her neck is wet with sweat and I drag my nails down the thin skin until I feel the shallow hollow at the base of her throat. I kiss her there before licking her collarbone, coating my tongue in her salty taste.

She exhales a burning breath into the night, arches her back and presses my face into her chest. I lift her off her feet and her legs slip around me as if they've been there before.

Her mouth locks onto mine and it feels as if hours elapse before I lower her, legs dangling over the earth and arms still clamped around my neck. Even while her feet find the floor we do not let each other go.

Ana throws her head back and I catch her curls in my fingers and sweep them off her forehead.

She looks up at me through hooded eyes, but she stares too long and her mouth forms a soft O. I see the muscles in her cheeks twitch.

"What's wrong?" I ask, although I know what she's seeing.

I tell myself that I am a Good Person and that I brought a woman with me for a romantic adventure and I'm going to take care of her. If Ana wants to go back, we can go right now.

She looks around and sees the bird vines strangling the plants and, in the distance, the engorged roots of the silk cotton tree fissuring the earth.

"Where are we?" she asks.

"The Gardens," I reply.

But she knows – and I know – that this place is not the Gardens.

Ana looks behind her. "There's no one there," I say, but I don't know if the words will comfort her.

She cranes her neck and I know she's listening for the sounds of the city. I listen too, almost hoping that Port of Spain will pierce this nowhere place and insist that life is chrome and glass and an endless array of machines instead of soft soil and darkness and parasitic plants.

Ana is on the tips of her toes as if she is about to run.

"But run where?" I ask.

Her body lurches and I feel the awful rending inside me. Me. He – wearing my skin and speaking my voice.

Ana turns, eyes squinting in the darkness, hands flailing as if she can catch safety. She runs away from us and my heart breaks because she is so slow.

I try to force my mouth open. To say we can go back. But I know, I always know, what is going to happen.

He makes my hand a fist. Ana's smell drenches everything she touches.

His legs coil before releasing. Saliva coats his gums and lubricates his throat.

Ana's voice eviscerates the night.

Why didn't you scream sooner? I want to ask her. *You barely know me; why did you come?*

The air stings our eyes. We know this place; we weave between the silk cotton roots where Ana stumbles. We break through the dying bougainvillea bushes.

She whirls around. Her legs quiver and she staggers.

He doesn't want it like this – he wants a chase. He stops. Waits.

She doesn't want to turn her back on him but she cannot bear to look any more. She is shaking so hard I wonder whether she can run at all.

She trots backwards; finally, desperately swivels. Her little legs pump and her rabbit-breathing punctuates the midnight.

Too slow.

I hate him. Hate myself. Want to make a noose out of the bird vines and let this be the end of it here.

He waits until she is far enough. Then he unleashes the speed. Like a bullet from a gun.

Ana's hair is rough in his hands. He forces her open mouth into the soil. Sinks his knee into the small of her back. Twists her wrists so that their soft underside is open to him.

I cannot look. Draw the curtain. Turn away.

★

One of Makedo's horns has become unglued and he is pacing backstage, anxiously trying to stick it back onto his head.

"Don't drip your blasted Jab Jab grease on my pitchfork!" one of the Blue Devils shouts.

"Boy, what your pitchfork doing just lying on the ground?" Makedo retorts.

Keston Victor, late as always, careens into the room. He almost collides with Gabriella Galloway, who is pale after throwing up in the bathroom for an hour before the show.

"Blasted Victor," the Blue Devils mutter.

Keston Victor ignores them and claws the shirt off his back, throws his jeans into a heap and digs his hands deep into the blue paint.

The new Pierrot Grenade is not nearly as good as Ana. She's still in her fluorescent stripes but even in that costume, she seems to recede into the wall.

I pull my hat low over my eyes. The belt of skulls around my waist rattles as I walk to the wings.

I check my left glove to make sure it's hiding the newest bruise on my wrist. I really don't want to hear another one of Makedo's lectures about liver disease.

"Knock them dead!" one of the Dame Lorraines whispers to

me. I incline my head in her direction. Her skin is like honey still wetly dark in the comb.

I hear the audience, shifting and murmuring. I rise to meet the Robber. Me. He. We're ready for the stage. The theatre lights are clamouring for a performance and this is my only opportunity to tell my story. I stretch my shoulders and let my steps become the Robber strut.

"Moon swallow sun, pelt the whole world into midnight. Trees tear open. Spirits bleed back into earth, teeming and screaming.

"Hell split to the deepest pit. I rise, storm without form. The last word Lucifer heard was my name – a sound so terrible it stop he ear so that now the Devil sit in silence because I come to master the master.

"This country have no hangman, but I am its Executioner.

"My house build with bones of men who will never have no grave. I pluck women like goose and the only juice I drink is their blood, boiling hotter than mortal man can tolerate.

"Lesser executioners leave you in shallow grave, but when I done, it will have no body to bury and your ashes go float forever – soul without home, death without life.

"Remember I am the one man make without fear. And if a Mocking Pretender like you dare to challenge me, the last sight you see is my eyes, dark and old, like soucouyant soul. The last voice you hear is mine – plunder and thunder. The last word you know is my name.

"Then you hear nothing. See nothing. Know nothing.

"Trinidad, I walk on water to you. I turn the earth in my palm. But I reach. I here. I hungry."

Trinidad, I walk on water to you. I turn the earth in my palm. But I reach. I here. I hungry.

THE ONE NIGHT STAND

He wakes up alone. The Saturday sounds seep through his blackout curtains. His neighbour is training her dog. "Down boy!" she shouts.

The woman walks into the room wrapped in a towel. The grey handle of his toothbrush is wedged between her teeth and specks of white foam dot her lips.

"You're using my toothbrush," he says.

"I couldn't find anozzer one," she says.

It's going straight in the bin when she leaves.

A one-night stand. Yes, God! Jackhammer sex – that's one thing, but to use someone else's toothbrush is an invasion of their privacy.

She walks back to the bathroom and he hears her spit. He fishes on the floor until he finds last night's boxers.

"What do you want for breakfast?" she calls from the bathroom. As if they are longtime lovers.

"There may be some eggs," he says, doubting their existence.

"I'll make do. Can I borrow one of your T-shirts?"

"Take one of the gym shirts. They're in the second cupboard in the walk-in closet, third row."

He hears her shuffling about, then she says, "*I like my women like I like my coffee. Ground up and in the freezer.*" It's his white shirt emblazoned with blood-red writing:

"Do you like your women like you like your coffee?"

"I don't think it's possible to choke coffee until it stops screaming," he says.

She laughs. "Oh! You're one of those!"

She comes in, raises her arms and twirls so that the T-shirt rises over her hips. Halfway through the spin she looks down at herself, as if her spottily shaved genitals are the most hypnotising thing in the world.

He doesn't respond.

"OK, Mr Sleepy," she says. She kisses him on the cheek, a rookie press of her lips, before walking downstairs.

In his bathroom, he sees that she's flecked his mirror with white globs of toothpaste and saliva – like a child who hasn't learnt to brush her teeth carefully, and spit in the sink. This is why he doesn't usually bring women to his apartment. Or one of the reasons. The maid won't be here until Tuesday. He spritzes the mirror with cleaning solution, then wipes it with a chamois cloth.

He doesn't like her in his kitchen alone. He goes downstairs.

"Your fridge is sorely lacking in eggs," she chirps.

"I don't usually cook breakfast."

"Well, I hope you enjoy bacon, slightly burnt toast and leftover potato au gratin."

"I don't imagine I will, but we'll see."

Against the backdrop of his quartz and chrome kitchen, every colour on her skin is magnified: purple half-moons of eyeliner smudged onto her face, a blue scar bleeding across her wrist. Her bare brown legs, her fun-house fattened thighs are reflected in his refrigerator and the shiny side of his oven.

When he was at university abroad he occasionally had women stay the night. The mornings-after had never been memories to relish. Often, they'd both been so hungover that between them there was only a smudged recollection of what had occurred: her high-pitched howls in piddling imitations of internet porn, choking if she was up for it. Or sometimes if she wasn't.

He'd given that up when he moved back home. Hotels were

better. Even the back seat of his car, although he loves his black Jaguar with a passion he rarely feels for people, and worries about soiling it. Still, a car has the advantage of ensuring that the woman is gone by morning.

She pulls the potatoes out of the microwave and tests them by holding her palms over the plate. Like a waitress, she brings the hodgepodge of food over to the breakfast nook. She's even dredged two glasses of orange juice from a near-empty carton.

He thinks unhappily of her bare ass on his pure white cushions. Though the interior decorator had advised that pure white was too stark for the décor – she'd suggested off white and eggshell for a homier feel – he's never considered "homey" a goal worth striving for. He'd gone with a pure white look, like a canvas for the view of the Gulf of Paria through his big French windows. Below them, the sea shudders and swells.

"Do you have plans for the rest of the day?" she asks.

He spreads some potato on toast and takes a bite. Woeful. "I have some work to do."

"Oh! What do you do?"

"Business development executive."

"Hence the house." She spreads her arms wide, as if she can touch the Austyn grey cashmere curtains in the living room, the African blackwood table, the orange roses and white cymbidium orchids arranged to spill out of opposite sides of a glass vase.

He nods. If he stays quiet, he's practically inviting her to ask him more. "What do you do?"

She lays her knife and fork down as if she needs both hands to answer. "I work at TTRCC."

The Trinidad and Tobago Rape Crisis Centre? It's too ridiculous.

"We're an NGO that – "

"Yes, I know." He can't resist. "Don't they teach their staff techniques to avoid assault? Like not letting strange men buy them drinks?"

She blushes.

"And you're still here? I could be anybody."

"But you're not."

"Why not?"

She smiles. "You're a nice guy."

"That's your conclusion on the balance of evidence?"

"You made sure to ask permission…"

How low the bar has been set for men.

"Sweetheart, look at the shirt you're wearing."

"It's a joke."

"Is it?"

She looks around with a hand on her throat as if they're in a movie. Maybe the lowest piano notes will begin playing and her eyes will alight on *The Silence of the Lambs* with Hannibal Lecter's face answering her question.

It's the learned, cinematic gesture that makes him wonder. "How old are you?"

"Twenty-four."

He'd expected her to lie about her age, but that seems about right.

She breaks off a sliver of bacon and nibbles. "So, when do you want me to clear out of here?"

Good. One way or another, she's finally gotten the message. "As soon as you're done."

She blinks, seems to push the comment to the side. "Of course. You have a lot to do." Again, it's the tone of someone who knows him, who knows exactly what his work entails. Is it part of her fantasy? That she's his girlfriend and soon she'll be back in his car or his house and he'll be back in her.

Neither of them says anything. He decides that he doesn't owe her the show of eating this slop and dumps the rest in the bin.

"I'm going to shower. I can give you a lift to where you're going when I'm done."

Even after he's bathed and dressed, she's only just stripping off his T-shirt. She puts on the baby-blue bra from the night before, her fingers fumbling. He walks up to her and snaps the bra shut. She looks hurt by the abruptness of the gesture.

Is it because – in her view of men – they're always slobbering for sex?

Her dress from last night was a second-skin number and he sees she feels foolish stepping into it at this hour. She slips her feet into sparkling stilettos.

"Where are you going?" he asks as they walk downstairs.

"Ellerslie Plaza."

Very good. She's willing to risk the walk of shame so that he won't have her home address. So she's not a total twit.

The Jaguar purrs to life. He hears Lorraine next door imploring her untrainable basset hound to heel. They glide out of the garage.

Outside the car, Sahara dust swirls. The clouded sky, like a leaden lid hammered over the island, casts everything in shadow.

She shifts, remarking on the recent rainy weather. If they didn't fuck one last time, at least they put on the appearance of a couple settled into comfort. Silence descends on them.

His phone rings over the Jaguar's Bluetooth. His mother.

"Are you going to answer it?"

"I'll call back."

Her hand darts out and she stabs the answer button.

"Rafe?" his mother asks.

"Little busy, Mom. Talk quickly."

"Just calling to let you know it's fish for lunch tomorrow, dear. Do you remember the dry Pinot Grigio you bought last time, just a hint of pear?"

His mother would drink piss if he put it in a bottle with a cork and told her it was 14%. "I'll get another one," he says, with no intention of trying.

"That's lovely! Melanie is bringing her latest boyfriend. This one is an architect, I think. I don't suppose you – "

He hangs up. He knows what she is going to say: she doesn't suppose he has a female friend he would like to bring? It breaks her heart to see him so busy with work all the time. If he were alone they would have had their usual spat where she would lament everything – from the hours he spends in front his computer to his unborn children. She would tell him again the story of poor Uncle Edward who rose to the dizzying height of regional CEO of Microsoft but never got married. And where was Uncle Edward now? Dead from testicular cancer at forty-three, with no one to clean his grave on All Souls Day.

Her worries would be blunted by his Sunday wine offering, until the next day. The relentless attempts of his sister, Melanie, to amount to nothing more than a barely-literate housewife never broke his mother's heart. But his refusal to indulge in the casual dating expected of men his age, before bumbling into marriage – *that* was a tragedy.

He resents the familiar way this woman answered his phone. But he doesn't want her to see she's capable of getting a reaction from him.

Privately, he thinks of Sundays with his family as the tenth circle of Dante's hell, reserved for sons saddled with spectacular failures. Yet, Melanie did not just do badly at school. She failed dramatically in subjects like English where just writing your name on a paper got you at least five percent.

"If this were another life, maybe you and I could go to that lunch together," the woman says.

He waits, expecting her to explain. But she remains silent, preening in the seat next to him.

"You wouldn't want to come," he says.

"It'll get your mother off your back," she says. She sounds hopeful.

Would it? What if he were to show up with this woman at the

family lunch? It would almost be worth it if his mother were struck speechless. It would certainly put an end to her pussy-footing around the issue of his sexuality. She would wait until they were alone and insinuate that maybe... ah... there was *someone* he could invite... not that his father would... ah... well everyone knows that Nick Stevenson's son is... ah... was there *someone*?

What was there about this wreck of a morning that has made this woman want to spend more time with him?

This, he decides, is the problem with women today. They've gorged on Facebook and Instagram where emotions are performative. They're bludgeoned by books and TV series and movies that celebrate men's borderline sociopathic behaviour. Men are raised to be monsters and if they manage to rein in the worst parts of themselves, that's all women can expect. These women will grasp at any fragment of humanity to hold it up as evidence of romance. They're the lead actress in a world where a one-night stand blooms into love in a couple of days.

The steering wheel slides through his hands as the car turns towards the Plaza. "What will I tell them when you don't show up to the next family lunch?" he says.

"I'm sure you can think of something."

★

Sunday sees them driving to his parents'. She's holding a Riesling in her lap as if it's a baby. "Is my dress OK?" she asks.

It actually is. She's wearing a peach one-shoulder number with a Grecian sort of drape.

"I was pleasantly surprised," he says.

She whacks his shoulder. "You're going to have to be nicer to me if your parents are going to believe we're lovers."

"Aren't we?"

She likes that.

The guard opens his parents' gate when they see the car. She whistles. "And I thought *your* house was nice."

The whole setup is too faux-English for him. The stone house and the manicured rosebushes try too hard. His parents' gardeners have purged the yard of anything too local. Hibiscuses survive – probably because they're gaudy and red like roses. But the lesser flowers – the butterfly jasmine and ixora – are weeded out if they ever take root.

He parks. "I'll need a couple minutes to let them know you're with me."

"You didn't call your mother back?" she asks.

Oh? She's nervous now.

He grabs the neck of the bottle. "It'll be fine."

"Darling," his mother says, prying the Riesling from his fingers. "Perfect! I simply must get the cork off!"

His father claps him on the shoulder and asks halfheartedly the usual question: "How's the office, son?"

He sees Melanie, standing too close to a mop of a blond hair in an Armani Exchange shirt who must be the architect.

His mother swans back into the room, glass in hand. "Rafe, this is Justin," she says. "He's the architect working on the new developments in Lange Park."

"Delighted," he says.

Melanie keeps her arm around Justin's waist through their handshake. She can't tear her eyes away from him.

"Justin is Genevieve Hunte's cousin. You remember Genevieve?" his mother asks.

"Barely," he says. "But I do have a slight wrench to throw into today's plans."

"Let me guess, you have to leave early to work, even though it's a Sunday," Melanie says. She rolls her eyes at Justin. It's clear she's already spinning stories about big brother, the workaholic. She's never missed an opportunity to shit all over him.

"Actually, I finally took up the invitation to bring someone to lunch," he says.

His mother blinks rapidly. "Someone?"

She appears in the doorway with the midday sun behind her. "I was just trying to explain my bad manners," he says to her. "These are my parents, Juliette and Vincent; my sister, Melanie; and Justin."

"So pleased to meet you," she says to his family. "And you must be the architect," she says to Justin.

"Apparently he's working on some new developments in Lange Park."

His family stand like wax statues.

"This is Jennifer," he says.

She steps over and touches his elbow. "I can't believe you didn't tell anyone I was coming."

His mother hears the familiar way she talks to him. Sees the way her hand cups his elbow. She shakes her head like a woman waking up. She assesses the classy cut of Jennifer's peach dress, made even better by its favourable comparison to the girlish-sexiness of Melanie's crop top. She sees Jennifer's straight black hair, small waist, the subtle swell of her hips. She sees the pale pink studs in her ears and the slim silver watch on her wrist. "*Welcome* to lunch, my dear," she coos.

The first course is a black kale and olive salad soaked in sherry vinegar. "So tell me, how did you two meet?" his mother asks.

Jennifer smiles at him like the story's a secret.

"At a party," he says.

"You go to parties?" Melanie demands. Her face is puffy with petulance. "I remember your form six graduation and you didn't put a toe on the dance floor." She smirks at their father as if this is somehow a joke between them.

"He hasn't been to one since we met," Jennifer fake-whispers to Melanie in a conspiratorial tone. "I can't deal with all the other women frothing at the mouth when they see him."

His father looks prouder than when Rafe was accepted into Oxford.

"And how did you two meet?" Jennifer asks Melanie. Her voice is syrup.

His mother turns to the architect who, until that point, may as well not have been at the table.

Melanie launches into a long story, the crux of which is they met in the gym. Under the table, Jennifer curls her inner ankle around his heel. When no one is looking, he digs the tines of his fork into her thigh.

Melanie has somehow worked into the story the number of bench presses the architect can do. His mother chews the kale like cud. "Very nice dear," she says. "Jennifer, what do you do?"

"She's a girl who cares more about charity than money," he says.

Jennifer swats his hand. "I work at the T&T Rape Crisis Centre."

He spears an olive. "Great lunch conversation, *babe*."

"It's an important issue," she says. "There's been this recent surge of violence against women, and we need to make sure that women speak up."

"So, you think the victims *can* speak up?"

"Of course, three in four victims know the accuser and if they feel empowered to go to the police and name him…"

"Right. Because the police are upstanding moral pillars and models of efficiency to boot."

"So, what do you think women should do, Mr Business Development Executive? I bet you solve complex problems at work all the time."

"I think they should go to the shooting range, practice until they're a crack shot, and then take care of problems themselves."

He feels his family's eyes moving from him to her. "Anyway. We can talk more about it later," he says.

"Sorry," she mumbles.

"No, not at all," his father says. "It's a very noble job you're doing."

He offers to help his mother clear the first course. "Where have you been keeping her?" his mother asks as soon as they're in the kitchen.

"You're not going to expect this every weekend, are you?"

"No, Rafe, but you know I've tried to talk to you about the importance of companionship…"

"How many drinks have you had?"

"I just feel so happy. And I've been worrying about you so much. That's all." Her eyes are damp. She removes her glasses and dabs lightly. A couple of tears have oozed into the lines below her eyes.

He remembers a time when he was a teenager and he'd lied to her about being invited to a sleepover. Instead, he'd planned to spend the night walking around the neighbourhood and had an ambitious strategy to scale trees and spy on his neighbours, particularly Ariana Duval. He'd prepared a litany of answers should his mother ask about the sleepover. But she'd barely asked him anything.

"You? A sleepover?" she'd asked. "Oh, Rafe! We have to buy some board games for you to play with the other children!"

A week later, she'd dropped him, saddled with a stack of board games, at the mall, and when she'd asked to meet the other boys he'd shouted that he was fifteen and the other boys wouldn't be there with their mothers tagging along, at which point she'd backed off. But she'd peppered him with questions for months after the "sleepover". Did he want to invite the boys to his house? Maybe his father could drive them to the beach or take them down the islands on his boat?

He'd heard her crying to his father after none of these things had happened. "Our son! He has friends, Victor. We just need to show him how to be friendly."

And his father: "After those boys invited him once, you

think they'll want to do it again? You know what he's like. Leave it alone, Juliette."

They go back to the dining room with the fish. "It's lemon sole fillets with chipotle and ancho chilli recado and an avocado side salad," his mother announces.

He feels some of his familiar irritation with family lunches. He knows they're expected to ooh and ahh at whatever internet recipe she's translated onto the plate.

"Looks great, Mom!" Melanie says before tearing through the skin of the fish. She's barely glanced at the plate.

His father chimes in, like a clock that goes off every Sunday, with a "compliments to the chef".

"Mmm," says Jennifer. "Did you roast the garlic in the marinade?"

His mother turns to Jennifer. "Yes. I roasted it skin on for about twenty minutes. And then I soaked the chillies in boiling water."

"I have to try that," Jennifer says. "Poblanos are my go-to chillies, but these are delicious." She nudges him. "Rafe, you need to start stocking your fridge like your Mom."

He shakes his head, but he has to admire how she's doing it.

"Do you know what we had for breakfast yesterday?" she asks his family. "Toast, bacon and leftover potatoes!"

"I know I raised my son better than that," his mother says. Actually, it sounds like a question.

"Typical Rafe," Melanie says to the architect, but loud enough for the rest of the table to hear. "Finally gets a girlfriend and can't even keep food in his fridge for her."

All his childhood, he'd longed for his parents to correct these outbursts.

His mother looks outside, preparing to make a pronouncement on the weather.

"We had such a good time the night before that I didn't mind," Jennifer says to him, but loud enough for everyone else to hear.

For the first time in his life, he understands why men brag about women.

"What did you do the night before?" Melanie demands.

"The usual," Jennifer says. "A game of Scrabble followed by prayer and reflection."

His father snorts. The snorts bubble into laughter.

Melanie, not used to having their parents on his side, looks to their mother. But she's also smiling at Jennifer as if to say, *You are the woman who noticed I roasted the garlic in my sauce and the martyr who's dating my son; I'll allow it.*

★

They leave holding hands but she lets go once they're in the garage. He drives the car eastwards to Ellerslie Plaza.

"They're not so bad," she says.

"You don't have to pretend anymore."

The sea rolls into view, made almost silver by the sun. The Jaguar glides over the gentle Carenage hills as they push past apartment buildings and then Vie de France, still swollen with Sunday brunchers.

"What do you usually do after family lunch? Nice long nap?"

"No."

He sees children kicking a football in the park. Men are playing all fours on top of a beer cooler. Women stand in small circles chatting, their hands curled around café latte cups.

She shifts in her seat. "You didn't even ask me why I came."

"Why did you come?"

Unusually for him, he's interested in the answer. Although, he supposes, she could have made up her mind to try to keep him after seeing his house and his car.

"I like you. Like, you put on this facade of toughness, but I can tell what you're really like."

He wishes she hadn't given a generic Rom Com answer. Her performance at lunch made him expect better.

"So I'm a tough guy with a heart of gold."

If she hears his tone, she ignores it. "I think that's closer to the truth than you'd like to admit."

The road becomes pockmarked with potholes. He slows his car.

"In my family, we didn't get on so well," she tells him. "I ate lunch in my room a lot. Even now, I rent a place and I still eat lunch on my bed. A bad habit I guess." She swivels so that she's facing him. Her knee is almost touching the gearstick. "My parents used to have these loud fights. My mom was from Romania and she just used to be cooped up in the house all day and she would be simmering like one of those pots. And as soon as my dad got home, it would start. Like, if he parked his car crooked she would tell him to straighten up, or if he didn't wipe his feet before coming in, she'd tell him she couldn't continue to live like this."

She keeps looking at him. He turns up the radio.

A soprano throb fills the car.

It's you, babe
And I'm a sucker for the way that you move, babe
And I could try to run, but it would be useless
You're to blame
Just one hit of you, I knew I'll never be the same

Her cheeks redden. She thinks he did it on purpose. That he was listening to the radio and picked his spot.

He lowers the volume.

"You're projecting your expectations onto me. I could still be anyone."

"So you're a psychopath? A high-functioning sociopath? A serial killer? I doubt any of those people care so much about what their mothers think."

"I don't care."

"Then what was today about?"

When he was seventeen, already Oxford-bound and sulking

around the neighbourhood to get away from his parents, he'd run into Ariana Duval. She'd asked him if he wanted to come inside for fresh-squeezed orange juice and he'd accepted. It would have been better to say no. The ordinariness of Ariana, her vapid conversation on celebrities, the eager-puppy way she kept brushing against him as if he always happened to be in her way – all of it made him realise that sometimes women are better imagined than experienced. In his mind, Ariana was a well-read young lady, comfortable with silence but with a dirty mind and a sarcastic streak. There she was blathering on about metallic lipstick being in this season.

His first kiss tasted of too-sweet orange juice, punctuated by lurid, slurping sounds as she sucked his bottom lip before releasing it with a smack. He'd thought that if this didn't improve it might well be his last kiss. In a bid to salvage something, he'd snatched a cutting board from the counter and paddled Ariana on her ass. She'd tensed up right away, but then smothered that with a contrived throaty laugh. By then he knew he wouldn't be back to the Duvals for more kissing.

What if he were to follow Jennifer's lead and tell stories about his childhood. Would she still think he was the bad boy who just needs some love?

"Rafe?" Jennifer asks in a softer tone.

"Can I help you?"

A cluster of ginger lilies are growing on the roadside, their petals a mawkish maroon.

"Did you –" She adjusts the drape of her dress, smooths the skirt. "Did you have a good time today?"

He is about to say, no. A good time? With his family? With her?

He remembers the way she one-upped Melanie. The way she introduced the topic of female victimhood, of all things, at lunch and instead of offering comments on the weather, had gotten his family interested. Had gotten *him* interested.

"It wasn't the worst family lunch I ever attended."

She smiles slightly. "I had a good time too."

The sunlight catches the scar on her wrist. He remembers giving it to her the night they met. The extra pressure. Had it hurt too much? Just the right amount?

As they drive into Maraval, Ellerslie Plaza comes into view, pink and peach, with walls that are – inexplicably to him – a dark, mossy green. The Plaza has always seemed ugly but today it looks even worse than usual – geometric squares of colour that have no business being on the same building.

He can't imagine that she's going to let him just drop her here. How far does she live, in this apartment where the bedroom doubles as the dining room?

He puts on his indicator and begins to slow down. "This is it."

He hears the car before he sees it. A silver Nissan comes careening around the corner, engine coughing, tyres screeching. The car is right behind them but shows no sign of slowing. He forces the Jaguar up onto the pavement and throws his arm across her. The bottom of the Jaguar crashes into the curb and bounces up. The Nissan's wing mirror passes within an inch of his as the car speeds past.

They exhale. His arm is still holding her in place.

"Who needs airbags?" she asks, tapping his wrist. "Did he scratch your car?"

He'd been about to ask if she were OK.

He guides the Jaguar back onto the road. He brings the wing mirror in and looks for scratches.

"No."

"Thank you, Rafe," she says. Her voice is cool and easy.

Thank you for lunch? For pulling aside that quickly? For a protective gesture that he didn't even know he had in him?

"You're welcome."

He waits for her pitch. Is she going to ask that he drop her home, with the implication that he can come in? Explain that his gesture shows that he does, in fact, have a heart of gold?

She pulls her purse in her lap.

What? No invitation? Not even a hint for him to pick up on? A suggestion? Wasn't that why she came?

The door clicks as she unlocks it. She kisses him on the cheek. She's wearing the same perfume as two nights ago – grapefruit, jasmine, coconut base notes. He feels the gentle press of her hand on his shoulder and then she's stepping outside.

"What are you doing Saturday?" he asks.

ACKNOWLEDGEMENTS

So many people have done so many things to help me write and publish this book.

Thank you to the wonderful folks at Peepal Tree Press: Jeremy Poynting, Hannah Bannister and Jacob Ross. You have done so much for these stories.

Thank you to the team at the NGC Bocas Lit Fest: Nicholas Laughlin and Anna Lucie-Smith, without you this collection could have remained a manuscript.

My literary family at the People's Republic of Writing (PROW) has read and re-read these stories and many worse ones that didn't make it to the collection. Thank you, Caroline Mackenzie and Andre Bagoo, the best friends and sources of inspiration an author could ask for.

Thank you to the people who could have been doing almost anything in the world, but who read early drafts of these stories instead: Sharon Millar, Hema Son Son and Nirad Tewarie. Your feedback has been invaluable

Thank you to the friends who believed in this book before I'd written a single story. Maria Huggins, Paige Andrew, Damir Ali and Anthony Medina – it means the world.

Thank you to Kevin Huggins – not just for the cover picture and headshot – but for all his beautiful photos.

There are no words to adequately thank Andrew Deane for his love, support and cooking. He's also a hell of a first editor.

Always, thank you to my family. Yvonne and David Mc Ivor. Beverly and Gordon Deane. Keegan Forde. Cynthia Andrew, who told me bedtime stories since before I can remember. My father, Herman Lee King, who always believed in my education. My brother, Brandon Mc Ivor, not just a brilliant writer but a brilliant man. And my mother, Louana Mc Ivor, the strongest woman I know.

Four of these stories were published previously, in slightly different forms:

"The Boss" – First published in *adda*, 2018 by Commonwealth Writers, the cultural initiative of the Commonwealth Foundation, London, UK. www.addamagazine.com www.commonwealthwriters.org. Finalist for the 2018 Commonwealth Short Story Prize

"Things We Do Not Say" – First published in *The Caribbean Writer Volume 31,* 2017. http://www.thecaribbeanwriter.org/.

"Ophelia" – First published in *adda*, 2016 by Commonwealth Writers, the cultural initiative of the Commonwealth Foundation, London, UK. www.addamagazine.com www.commonwealthwriters.org.

"Kristoff and Bonnie" – First published in *The Caribbean Writer Volume 29,* 2015. Winner of The David Hough Literary Prize, 2015. http://www.thecaribbeanwriter.org/.

ABOUT THE AUTHOR

Breanne Mc Ivor was born and raised in west Trinidad. She studied English at the Universities of Cambridge and Edinburgh before returning home. She has been shortlisted for the Commonwealth Short Story Prize, the Glimmer Train Fiction Open, the Fish One-Page Prize and the Derek Walcott Writing Prize. In 2015, she won The Caribbean Writer's David Hough Literary Prize. *Where There Are Monsters* is her first short story collection.